Adam launched his campaign against Jenna

His first success came with a comment he made. Her laugh was spontaneous—and sexy as hell. It rattled him for a moment, until he reminded himself who she was and why he was there.

The next time, he arrived armed with the determination to break through that glacial wall she was hiding behind—and spurred by a compulsion to prove that he could.

But the sight of her, sitting there under the blazing sun, hugging her arms as if she were chilled to the bone, brought him up short. She looked lost... forlorn. Scared.

He impatiently dismissed the impressions. It had to be an illusion, a trick of his mind. That deceptively sweet, innocent face of hers could make a man imagine all sorts of nonsense.

ABOUT THE AUTHOR

The idea for *The Woman in the Mirror* came to Lynn Turner after watching a television talk show that featured women who had staged their own deaths and assumed new identities. Lynn, her husband and their two sons live in Mount Vernon, Indiana, where she assumes "the identity of a non-English-speaking foreign-exchange student when someone tries to sell me aluminum siding over the phone."

Books by Lynn Turner

Don't miss any of our special offers. Write to us at the following address for information on our newest releases.

Harlequin Reader Service
901 Fuhrmann Blvd., P.O. Box 1397, Buffalo, NY 14240
Canadian address: P.O. Box 603,
Fort Erie, Ont. L2A 5X3

The Woman in the Mirror

Lynn Turner

Harlequin Books

TORONTO • NEW YORK • LONDON
AMSTERDAM • PARIS • SYDNEY • HAMBURG
STOCKHOLM • ATHENS • TOKYO • MILAN
MADRID • WARSAW • BUDAPEST • AUCKLAND

ISBN 0-373-22268-8

THE WOMAN IN THE MIRROR

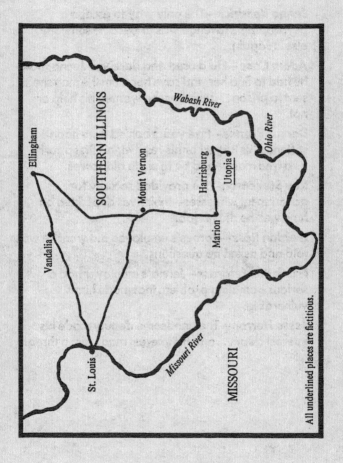

Wabash River

Ohio River

Ellingham

SOUTHERN ILLINOIS

Mount Vernon

Harrisburg

Utopia

Vandalia

Marion

Missouri River

St. Louis

MISSOURI

All underlined places are fictitious.

CAST OF CHARACTERS

Jenna Kendrick—The only way to escape a psychopath's revenge was to become someone else . . . again.

Adam Case—He'd used and deceived Jenna; now he had to find her and save her from the man she'd sent to prison . . . whether she wanted his help or not.

Dennis Barnes—Five years behind bars hadn't softened his hatred or his resolve; his first priority as a free man would be to settle old scores.

Roy Stevenson—He provided security for government witnesses—their lives depended on how well he did his job.

Gordon Ross—Barnes's employee did what he was told and asked no questions.

Frank Pendergrass—Jenna's employer had a serious gambling problem that made him vulnerable.

Jesse Herron—The handsome deputy made his interest clear . . . and his interest made him a threat.

Prologue

Barnes was taken to the ten-by-ten-foot conference room early and left to cool his heels for fifteen minutes before his attorney arrived. He stoically endured the wait on a hard wooden chair, his strong, blunt hands folded on the scarred tabletop. He was seldom called upon to exercise patience. Even in this federal prison, others waited for Dennis Barnes, and they did so without complaint.

The blue chambray shirt and navy cotton trousers he wore were custom-made, tailored to fit his compact six-foot frame as perfectly as the Cerruti and Armani clothing that crowded his cavernous closets in Maryland and California and Saint-Tropez. At least he wouldn't have to shop for clothes when he left this place. He was confident that nothing would require alteration. His body had retained its trim dimensions, thanks to regular workouts and an occasional five rounds with a former middleweight contender sharing his cell block.

His hair was shorter than he liked, and inexpertly cut, but that was a minor aggravation which would soon cease to be of concern. He spread his hands on the table and frowned. The Rolex watch and heavy gold signet ring he'd been wearing when he arrived five years ago were locked away in a safe somewhere in the gray stone bowels of the prison complex, presumably in proximity to the warden's office. It wasn't the absence of these items that prompted Barnes's frown, though, but the state of his hands.

The calluses and stained, jagged nails were unwelcome reminders of a past he'd fought like a demon to put behind him, to expunge as if it had never happened. It had taken years, not to mention large sums of untraceable cash and the discreet use of blackmail and extortion, but eventually he had erased all record of his personal history.

And then he'd created a new one to replace it—a fictitious biography which had allowed him to build an empire rivaling the world's largest corporations in scope and power. In time, the tentacles of his influence had penetrated the most exalted sanctums of business, finance and government. He had few enemies, because it was universally known that a word from Dennis Barnes could guarantee not only spectacular success but also utter, humiliating defeat.

He had made himself a king. A twentieth-century demigod.

And then *she* had betrayed him, and all his wealth and power hadn't been able to save him.

He unconsciously balled his hands into fists. An artery throbbed at his temple as the familiar impotent rage rose inside him. He still burned at the ignominy of having been brought down by a woman—and not a woman who wielded any power of her own, but an *employee,* a glorified errand girl! A cunning, deceitful little cipher, whose only value to anyone had been her association with him. And—this had been the final, intolerable insult—his own wife's sister.

Kendra Jenner. The name was a raw brand on his soul, both an epithet and an objective, the incentive that had made the past five years bearable. He had spent months planning his retribution. And now, finally, the waiting was almost at an end.

The heavy steel door on the far side of the room opened and Everett Whitledge entered. A uniformed guard followed the tall attorney inside and stationed himself against the wall as the door was closed and locked by a turnkey in the corridor beyond. The guard stared straight ahead, pretending disinterest, but Barnes knew that every syllable that was uttered during this meeting would be reported to the warden, who would in turn synopsize the conference for the U.S. attorney.

"Have you been waiting long?" Everett asked as he took a seat across the table.

Barnes moved one hand in a brusque, dismissive gesture. "It's a petty game they play, trying to provoke me into losing my temper."

Everett placed his attaché case on the table, opened it and removed a manila folder. "You'd think they'd have realized by now it can't be done," he murmured as he took a two-page computer printout from the folder. He slid the pages across the table. Barnes quickly scanned both, then returned them without comment.

"We're right on schedule," Everett said. "Your hearing is set for next Wednesday, 10:00 a.m. Everyone on the list will be there, plus a couple of people who've come forward on their own in the past several days."

Barnes nodded. He'd expected a few last-minute volunteers—people who might want favors once he was out. "And the matter I asked you to follow up on?" he asked quietly.

"No change," Everett replied. "As a matter of fact, I heard from your agent this afternoon, as I was about to leave the office. She assures me you shouldn't have any trouble dispensing with that old business."

Barnes propped his elbows on the table and rested his mouth against his linked hands. "Good," he said in the same subdued tone.

The pose was calculated to conceal his expression from the guard, but he knew Everett's shrewd courtroom gaze detected the hatred that blazed for a moment in his eyes.

"Good," he repeated even more softly as he lowered his hands. His intelligent hazel eyes were once more mirrors, reflecting rather than revealing. "Call her back right away, as soon as you leave here. Tell her the old business will be my first priority."

For a moment Everett Whitledge looked as if he might say something—perhaps offer an opinion or a bit of unsolicited advice. But then he lowered his gaze, replaced the folder in his attaché case and murmured a deferential "As you wish."

Chapter One

Jenna Kendrick smacked the alarm to silence its insistent buzzing, then lay back and stared blearily at the ceiling. Her eyeballs felt like they'd been scoured with sandpaper. Not the fine-grained emery-board variety, but the coarse, heavy-duty stuff that gouges and scars. She'd had maybe two hours' sleep, and that had been fitful, interrupted by terrifying dreams that catapulted her into consciousness and left her gasping and drenched with sweat, her heart knocking against her ribs.

Bright sunlight was assaulting the miniblinds at the eastern window, trying to prize open the dusky rose slats. Jenna wrestled with the desire to turn her back on the clock's glowing numerals, pull the covers over her head and close her eyes. She knew she'd be able to sleep, now that daylight had driven away the concealing shadows and the demons who inhabited them.

Unfortunately, she also knew that the shadows and the demons would be back the next night, and the next. Real, live demons weren't so easily vanquished.

And real jobs that provided real paychecks weren't so plentiful that she could afford to spend the day catching up on her sleep. Venting her frustration with a resentful groan, she fought free of the bedclothes and got up, shoving the snarled mass of her hair out of her face as she stumbled to the bathroom for a long, hot shower.

Forty minutes later she gunned her four-year-old Escort into the eastbound traffic on Manchester Avenue. Ahead, the top of the Gateway Arch proudly stood sentinel above a landscape of office buildings, hotels and banks. Her first sight of the Arch on the drive to work always lifted Jenna's spirits. Thankfully, today was no exception.

She'd first laid eyes on the futuristic landmark five years and three months ago. To her, the Arch had come to symbolize new beginnings, fresh starts...faith in the future. This morning she embraced the symbolism with a fervency that approached desperation.

As usual, the single-story building that housed Pendergrass and Son, Independent Insurance Agents and Realtors, was empty when Jenna arrived. She changed the thermostat from its overnight setting to activate the air-conditioning, started a pot of coffee, then went to her desk, sat down...and immediately decided she should have stayed in bed.

There in the middle of the blotter was the telephone-message slip that had started the emotional roller-coaster ride she'd been on for the past twenty or so hours. "Call your Uncle Roy, ASAP," Verda Young's tidy block letters instructed.

It wasn't the message, per se, that had triggered Jenna's first faint tingle of premonition. "Uncle Roy" frequently checked in with her—or up on her, she'd never been sure which—at work. If she was in a meeting or out running an errand when he called, a small blue message slip would be waiting when she returned to her desk.

It was the way Verda had virtually pounced on her the second she entered the building, combined with that imperative "ASAP," that had made her stomach churn and her heart suddenly pick up speed. This was only the second time in five years that one of Roy's messages had transmitted such a sense of urgency. The first time, he'd been trying to reach her to break the news that her sister and nephew had died in an airplane crash. To give him credit, he'd waited until she was seated in his comfortable, book-lined office to tell her. Not that she'd been in any shape to appreciate his kindness or compassion at the time. The news he'd had for her yesterday afternoon was almost as devastating, but this time he'd given it to her straight and all at once, over the phone.

"Your uncle called twice while you were at lunch," Verda had announced as she thrust the small slip of paper at Jenna. "He said it was extremely important and you should call him back as soon as you came in."

Jenna's murmured "Thanks" had, she hoped, covered a sudden anxiety that increased exponentially as she dialed Roy's number and was briefly put on hold by his secretary. As always, she was acutely aware that every word she said to him might be overheard by any of the half dozen people presently in the office.

"It's Jenna," she said as soon as he came on the line. "I received a message that you called while I was at lunch."

He hadn't wasted words or time, brutally destroying her illusion of safety and security in the space of five seconds.

"I got word this morning that Barnes has a parole hearing scheduled for next Wednesday."

The comfortably familiar sounds of the busy office were replaced by a low, droning buzz. The walls seemed to close in, and a suffocating pressure squeezed Jenna's chest. For a few seconds she'd thought she was going to pass out. It was the pain in her fingers, which gripped the telephone receiver so hard they'd started to throb, that finally caused her to inhale a jagged breath.

"Next Wednesday," she repeated, her voice thick with dread.

"Right. Listen, there's no reason to panic. The parole board will probably turn him down, and even if he wins an early parole he can't possibly know where you are."

The hollow assurances had provoked a hot surge of anger that temporarily overshadowed Jenna's fear. Either good old Uncle Roy's IQ had suddenly dropped a hundred points or he thought hers had. They both knew the things Dennis Barnes was capable of, the lengths to which he would go to settle a score.

"Save it, Roy," she said, keeping her tone low in case anyone was eavesdropping. "The people you work for might believe that. You might even believe it. But I know better than to take anything for granted where Dennis Barnes is concerned."

Roy had spent a couple more minutes trying to convince her there was nothing to worry about, but since he didn't sound all that convinced himself, nothing he said relieved Jenna's apprehension.

PENDERGRASS AND SON'S gray-tinted plate-glass door swung open and Liza Roper entered in a cloud of some exotic perfume, dragging Jenna back to the present. Liza was wearing emerald green today, a tailored shirtwaist dress and matching shoes. As always, she looked stunning. She paused a moment to flick a speck of lint from her bodice—it must have been lint; dandruff wouldn't dare contaminate Liza's magnificent dark auburn tresses—before greeting Jenna with a cheerful smile.

"Good morning!" she chirped. "Isn't it an absolutely gorgeous day?"

Jenna dredged up a smile in response. Usually Liza's congenital perkiness didn't bother her, but this morning it was a little hard to take. "Morning," she murmured. "Coffee should be ready in a few minutes."

"Great. I could use a shot of caffeine. I overslept and had to skip breakfast. Whose turn is it to pick up the donuts?"

"Frank's, I think," Jenna replied. The thought crossed her mind that if Liza had more than one cup of coffee, she'd be bouncing off the walls by nine-thirty.

Liza grimaced. "He always gets those gooey long johns that are stuffed with sugar and lard. We might as well shoot a couple pounds of cholesterol straight into our arteries." She started for her desk, then stopped, a concerned frown marring the smooth perfection of her forehead. "You okay, Jen? You look a little peaked."

Jenna summoned another smile and shook her head in denial. "I'm fine. I didn't sleep very well last night, that's all."

Liza's crystalline green eyes narrowed shrewdly. "Man trouble?"

"In a way," Jenna muttered.

She instantly regretted the dry response. No one she knew enjoyed girl talk—or, more to the point, man talk—more than Liza. Luckily Frank Pendergrass appeared, right on schedule, before Liza could start grilling her. Frank made a very effective diversion, huffing and puffing as he wrestled his substantial bulk through the door. He clutched his ancient, battered briefcase and the morning paper to his chest with one hand. On the other, a large white cardboard box balanced precariously.

"Somebody wanna give me a hand here?" he wheezed as the box tipped toward the floor.

Liza rescued it as it slid off his palm. "Long johns?" she guessed.

"Yeah, and a half dozen crullers. Any messages?"

"Nothing new," Jenna answered. "Just the stack I gave you yesterday afternoon." None of which he'd had time to do anything about, because he'd left the agency at three o'clock. Five minutes behind his father.

Liza sent her a wry look and headed for the kitchenette at the rear of the building. Frank informed her that he'd be leaving to show a property at ten and shambled off to his office, which was conveniently next to the kitchenette. A cynical smile tugging at her mouth, Jenna took a pencil from the mug next to her phone and placed a neat *X* in every block of time after ten on the calendar she kept for him. When had he made the appointment? she wondered as she replaced the pencil. After he left yesterday? And why hadn't he said which of their listings he was showing?

She stood up, intending to go ask him in case one of the agents had a potential buyer interested in the same property, but her phone rang. Then the rest of the staff started arriving, and by the time she got a couple of minutes free, Frank was gone.

At lunchtime, she walked to a nearby tavern and picked at a plate of corned beef hash. She remembered Frank's mysterious appointment and decided he was probably meeting his bookie or arranging a loan to pay off some losses. Everybody at the agency, with the apparent exception of his father, knew that Frank had a serious gambling problem.

The hash was terrible, dry and tasteless. Jenna gave up on it after a few bites and settled for making a meal of the cracked ice in her tea and a buttered roll. She wasn't really hungry, anyway; reliving yesterday's conversation with Roy had destroyed her appetite. Her fear of Dennis Barnes was threatening to take over her life again.

She wouldn't let it happen, damn it. She wouldn't let herself fall into the trap of imagining deceptions and assigning ulterior motives to everybody she came in contact with. . . including her own boss. A certain degree of caution made sense, but she had to control the inclination to see potential enemies everywhere she looked.

That guy, for instance. The lean, dark, cowboy type in the faded jeans and denim jacket sitting alone in the booth by the rear exit. He'd probably picked that booth because he was a private person and it was the only isolated table in the place, not because he always instinctively took a position near a window or door, with his back to the wall so he could keep an eye on everybody else.

Jenna's lips curved in a self-conscious smile as she reached for her wallet. She'd probably just satisfied her paranoia quota for the rest of the month.

ADAM GAVE HER TIME to reach the end of the block before he paid for his greasy cheeseburger and fries and followed her out of the tavern. He stayed with her long enough to be sure she went straight back to work, then found a pay phone and called the St. Louis office of the U.S. Marshals Service.

"She's nervous," he said as soon as Roy came on the line. "On edge. I think it's time to make my move."

Roy's response was typically sedate. "Of course she's nervous. She just found out about Barnes's hearing."

"Right." Cynicism sharpened Adam's indolent west Texas drawl. "And a pig just flew right over my head. A big blue porker with orange polka dots."

"Don't start," Roy murmured. "You know what I think—this will turn out to be a wild-goose chase, a waste of time and resources."

"Yeah, well, the people who pay our salaries don't agree. They suspect she's been in contact with Barnes all along."

"And we both know who originated that theory," Roy observed. "Take care, Adam. This is just another job. Don't turn it into a personal crusade."

Adam didn't react to the admonition until he'd hung up, and even then the only visible sign of his resentment was a slight tautening at the corners of his wide mouth. Jenna Kendrick, a.k.a. Kendra Jenner, was involved in Barnes's dirty business up to her eyeteeth. He knew it, and he was determined to prove it. And he could damn well do without any lectures about objectivity from Roy Stevenson. Apparently the woman had taken Roy in completely; he'd bought the whole honest-citizen-doing-her-moral-duty line.

Adam's mouth thinned in a grim smile as he headed for the parking lot around the corner to collect his car. She may have fooled Roy, but *he'd* had her number from the beginning. He knew Jenna Kendrick for the conniving little felon she was. And one way or another, he intended to see that both she and her lover Barnes paid for their crimes.

BY THE TIME SHE CLOSED the agency for the day, Jenna had a screaming tension headache. Her resolve not to see plots and conspirators everywhere had survived approximately fifteen minutes, the amount of time between her return from lunch and the appearance of the first walk-in customer of the day.

Evidently history did repeat itself, she reflected bleakly as she switched off the lights and fished her car keys out of her purse. Five years ago, when she'd first started work at the Pendergrass agency as receptionist-secretary, she'd been thrown into a panic every time a stranger entered the building.

She'd already been a nervous wreck when the Marshals Service relocated her to St. Louis, her stamina and whatever courage she'd had exhausted by the prolonged trial and the investigation preceding it. And then—as if God or the Fates or whoever suddenly decided she hadn't been knocked around enough—Roy Stevenson had called her to his office that sweltering August afternoon to tell her that the plane carrying her sister and six-year-old nephew had crashed and burned on takeoff. Mechanical failure, he'd assured her, as if that should soften the blow; no evidence of sabotage. There'd been fewer than ten survivors. Kayla and Thad weren't among them.

The news had almost destroyed Jenna. She'd voluntarily spent two years in hell—staying on as Barnes's secretary after she began to comprehend the extent of his criminal activities, risking her life to accumulate enough evidence to put him behind bars—all so Kayla would be able to escape the sadistic monster she'd married. And it had all been for nothing. Kayla and Thad never had a chance at the new life her testimony had bought them.

Despite the headache, Jenna didn't fully appreciate how tense she'd been until she was safely locked inside her small rented house in Maplewood. Suddenly every muscle in her body ached. Her pulse pounded like a sledgehammer at her temples and she started to tremble uncontrollably.

She'd never used tranquilizers, and the only alcohol in the house was the bottom third of a pint of gin left over from an office BYOB New Year's Eve party. She mixed a shot with some diet cola, threw in a couple of ice cubes and carried the glass through the house while she compulsively checked all the locks. The drink tasted like poison, and she ended up pouring half of it down the sink. But by the time she made her way back to the kitchen, she'd stopped shaking.

False courage, she told herself scornfully as she replaced the lethal-tasting drink with the club soda and fresh ice. When the booze wears off, you'll still be just as scared.

And for good reason. The inescapable fact was that she wouldn't feel safe as long as Dennis Barnes was on the same planet.

She was suddenly filled with rage. Damn him to hell! It had taken the better part of five years, but she'd finally settled into the new life the Marshals Service had given her. It fit like a pair of comfortably shabby old tennis shoes. She *was* Jenna Kendrick. More important, she *liked* Jenna Kendrick.

Dennis Barnes had already cost her one life. Damned if she'd just meekly surrender another. She carried the phone book to the table and opened it to the Security Systems section of the yellow pages.

Chapter Two

Adam had expected her to look older, or at least harder, more callous. He'd thought the five years she'd spent in exile, living a lie, would have left their mark. He was surprised—and if he was honest, a little resentful—that she hadn't lost the fresh-faced, virtuous look that had first aroused his suspicions. No woman who'd been involved with Dennis Barnes could be as innocent as Jenna Kendrick appeared.

And she *had* been involved with Barnes; Adam knew it in his gut. He'd known since the day five years ago when he learned that she had approached the attorney general's office out of the blue with an offer to testify against Barnes. Her cooperation had guaranteed a conviction on extortion and racketeering charges, but allowed Barnes to escape prosecution for the even more serious crimes Adam had been investigating.

Adam was determined to rectify the injustice her interference had caused. The word from the Justice Department's network of informants was that Barnes had called in every marker he held to buy an early parole. Eight days from now he would be a free man.

Adam had been sent to St. Louis to gather evidence that would help put Barnes back behind bars, for good this time. He was prepared to employ any and all available means to accomplish that objective, including using Jenna Kendrick.

He'd been there, observing from the back row every day of Barnes's trial. He'd seen the way Barnes watched her during her appearances as a material witness—he couldn't keep his eyes off her. Not that his obvious obsession was surprising. Kendra Jenner, soon to become Jenna Kendrick, had been a stunner by anyone's standards.

And still was, he acknowledged as he studied her from the doorway of a drugstore across the street. She was sitting at the receptionist's desk, just beyond the agency's entrance, so that he had an unobstructed view of her. She'd let her rich brown hair grow and wore more makeup now, but that improbably guileless, wholesome face could still cause a man's heart to stumble in amazement. She'd also added a few pounds since Barnes's trial, in all the right places. Five years ago she'd been slender as a reed; now her figure was more curvaceous, more womanly. Adam resented that, too, though he'd have been hard-pressed to say why.

Before he started across the street, he took a second or two to check out his own reflection in the drugstore window. His jeans were well-worn, beginning to fray a little at the hems where the denim rubbed against the equally worn leather of his tobacco-brown Western boots. The top two buttons of his pale blue shirt were casually undone, the sleeves rolled to his elbows. He'd do, he decided. No one, specifically Jenna Kendrick, would take one look and peg him as a senior investigator with the Organized Crime and Racketeering Section of the Justice Department's Criminal Division.

JENNA WAS FILLING IN for the receptionist, who was off having a plantar wart removed, when she heard the door open and then whoosh closed. She finished jotting down a message for one of the agents before lifting her head to murmur, "May I help you?"

As the last word left her mouth, she recognized the tall man on the other side of Verda's desk. The cowboy. The loner she'd indulged her paranoia by speculating about at lunch yesterday. Her guard came up in automatic reflex. The same stranger, first at the tavern and now here. It couldn't be a coincidence.

"I surely hope so," he replied.

His deep, languid drawl and howdy-ma'am smile perfectly complemented his wardrobe. For a moment she was tempted to go to the door to see if he'd left a horse hitched to one of the parking meters. But then the smile was replaced by a probing, squinty-eyed stare, and he remarked, "I know you from somewhere." He held up a hand before Jenna could decide how to respond. "No, don't tell me. It'll come to me in a minute. I never forget a face."

Hoping hers would be the exception, she gave him a perfunctory smile in return. *Okay, take it easy. Maybe it is just a coincidence that he's shown up two days in a row.*

It wasn't unusual for people to literally walk in off the street to inquire about insurance or real estate listings. Some had plucked the agency's name at random out of the yellow pages or the classified section of the newspaper. Others were referred by friends, neighbors or co-workers. Still others had taken one of the business cards the agents left in auto dealers' showrooms. And every now and then someone who'd just moved to the St. Louis area was directed to Pendergrass and Son by an out-of-state Realtor.

Jenna allowed herself to relax a little. So far as she knew, Dennis Barnes hadn't invested any of his dirty money in cattle ranches. Just in case, though, she concentrated on sending out cool, standoffish vibes, a skill she'd perfected over the years.

"Did you want to see someone about insurance coverage, or—"

"Got it!" he announced, cutting short the list of his options. His triumphant grin exposed a dimple in his right cheek and a set of strong, even white teeth, and folded the weathered lines at the corners of his eyes into accordion pleats. Jenna's heart gave a surprised little jump in response.

"The tavern, yesterday," he said. "You ordered a plate of hash, but you didn't finish it."

She responded without thinking. "It had the flavor and consistency of shredded newsprint."

"Can't have been worse than the cheeseburger and fries. If I'd had a vise and a drain pan, I could've saved the cost of my next oil change."

An appreciative laugh slipped out before Jenna could stop it. So much for being cool and standoffish, she thought wryly. "I think they're breaking in a new cook."

"Horses and boots get broken in," he observed. "Cooks should have to pass some kind of test before they're turned loose on paying customers—say, having to eat everything they ruin for a week. Insurance."

Captivated by that resonant, lazy drawl—damn, it certainly sounded authentic, sort of like Rip Torn at his most laid-back—Jenna was startled by the non sequitur. She blinked up at him in bewilderment.

"Sorry?"

"Insurance. That's what I came about. I need some." He flashed another dazzling grin and held out his hand. "Sorry, must've left my manners at home," he said as she automatically lifted her hand and let him enclose it in a firm, warm grip. "The name's Adam Case."

As Jenna withdrew her hand, she realized she was smiling back at him. She couldn't help it; he was as friendly and direct as a puppy. She dragged her thoughts back to business.

"What kind of policy did you have in mind, Mr. Case?"

"Renter's insurance, but I only need a short-term policy. Three months should do. I'm a free-lance travel writer," he explained. "I picked St. Louis as my base for a series I'm researching about lesser-known historic sites along the Mississippi."

ADAM CASE. THE NAME FIT him as perfectly as his snug, washed-out jeans. And he was actually wearing boots! An involuntary smile had tugged at her mouth when she'd noticed—honest-to-gosh cowboy boots, with scuffed pointy toes and run-down heels.

No doubt he was good at what he did. She could see him fitting in wherever he went, being instantly accepted by the innkeepers and restaurateurs and campground owners and travel agents he interviewed. He had a disarmingly straightforward manner, a droll sense of humor, and an innate charm that was damn near irresistible. Jenna had observed the effects of that charm when he came out of Frank's office twenty minutes later, a new renter's policy in hand. Frank had exerted himself to escort Adam three quarters of the way to the door—about fifteen feet farther than she'd ever seen him waddle for any other client—and pumped his arm vigorously in farewell before shambling back to his office.

All in all, Mr. Adam Case appeared to be quite a piece of work. He was also the most attractive man she'd met in years. So why, when he'd stopped at Verda's desk to entice her with another breathtaking grin and ask her to lunch, had she suddenly panicked and invented several errands that couldn't be postponed?

Because she was a neurotic idiot, she decided as she sat on a park bench in the shadow of the Arch and slurped at a melting frozen yogurt cone. She was aware of the train of coal barges being slowly prodded upriver by a stolid tug belching black smoke, and the shrieks of a group of preschoolers clambering over a nearby jungle gym, but only in a peripheral way. The gorgeous day was wasted on her. The brilliant, cloudless sky, the pungent, moldy smell of the river, the laughing children...even the Arch, the sight of which was usually enough to chase away her blues—all wasted, because she was too crippled by fear and distrust to appreciate any of it.

Maybe, she thought with a despondent sigh, this life was wasted on her.

If only it was the life she'd been born to, instead of a ready-made one she'd been grafted onto, like a shoot from a rose bush or an accident victim's kidney. She'd spent the better part of five years adjusting and adapting, remodeling herself to fit this new life the Witness Security Program had provided. In the main, she was satisfied with the results. Content, at least most of the time, if not deliriously happy. Her unusual circumstances made it difficult to form close or lasting friendships, but that hadn't been a terrible cross to bear, because she was by temperament and inclination a solitary person, anyway.

She probably would have continued to drift exactly as she had been, getting along and getting by, like virtually everyone she knew, for the rest of her life. A bit more reclusive than most, a little more wary of strangers, but in all other respects a typical, middle-class, single white female. But then two unconnected incidents—which had occurred, ironically, just a couple of days apart—had forced her to acknowledge that the life she'd been living was nothing but a sham, a pathetic imitation of the real thing.

No, she amended as she popped the last bit of sugar cone into her mouth. It hadn't been a couple of random happenings that suddenly yanked her fragile little world inside out, but two *people*. Two men, who had nothing in common and were, on the surface, at least, as different as night and day.

Dennis Barnes and Adam Case.

Barnes might be locked up in a federal prison a thousand miles away, but he was still controlling her. His domination was so complete that she hadn't dared admit that she was attracted to Adam Case, much less do anything about it. She couldn't risk letting him get too close. He might be exactly what he claimed to be, but he might just as easily have been sent by Barnes.

She knew Dennis Barnes, knew how his brilliant but twisted mind worked. It wasn't a question of *whether* he would take his revenge, but *when*. His parole hearing was scheduled for the following week. Considering the scope of his influence and the wealth at his disposal, Jenna fully expected that he would soon be a free man. He would probably come after her himself—he'd want the personal satisfaction. But first he would assign someone—maybe more than one someone—to watch her, report her habits and routine movements. Dennis Barnes never left anything to chance.

She hugged her arms as a chill spread through her. Oh, yes, he would come after her. And when he did, not even the U.S. Marshals Service would be able to protect her.

"Somebody just walk across your grave?"

The question probably would have sent her into cardiac arrest, if she hadn't instantly recognized that amiable drawl. She looked up in surprise as Adam Case stepped around the bench and sat down beside her. He'd discarded his denim jacket. A slim notebook protruded from the pocket of his shirt and a 35 mm camera hung around his neck. The camera's lens was uncapped.

"Didn't mean to scare you," he said with a low-wattage smile. "Get all your errands run?"

Jenna averted her eyes guiltily. "Yes. They didn't take quite as long as I expected." She paused a beat, then added, "You didn't scare me, I was just surprised to see you."

While it wasn't an outright lie, neither was it the unabridged truth. What was he doing here? Was she supposed to believe he'd just happened to mosey down to the riverfront to take some pictures while she was there?

And why not? her rational self retorted a moment later. Would you rather believe he's been following you—spying on you, snapping pictures and taking notes for Dennis Barnes?

He leaned back, resting his arms along the top of the bench and stretching his long legs out in front of him, feet crossed at the ankles, and squinted at the endless parade of traffic on the river.

"I didn't follow you," he remarked clairvoyantly. Jenna gave a startled jerk, which he politely ignored. "I've never seen the Arch up close, and I wanted to check out a couple of the stern-wheelers. They're smaller than I thought they'd be. Have you ever taken one of the day trips?"

"No," she murmured, grateful for the tactful change of subject. Was she that easy to read? "I always intended to, but somehow I never got around to it. I have gone up to the top of the Arch, though. It's quite a view."

He abruptly hauled his legs back in and sat up. "Great. You can be my tour guide."

Jenna turned her head and met his level, expectant gaze. Her heart thumped in alarm. "Now?"

"We're here," he said reasonably, inclining his head toward the Arch. "Makes more sense than coming back some other time. Unless you have to get back to work?"

She automatically glanced at her watch. "No, I still have almost half an hour."

What was she doing? she wondered with a sort of detached disbelief. She knew nothing whatsoever about the man, except for the scanty details he'd provided back at the agency, and that could have been a pack of lies. What if Dennis Barnes *had* sent him?

He must have sensed her hesitancy. He shifted position, turning sideways to face her. "Look, I'm not sure how I screwed up, but it's obvious I didn't make a dynamite first impression," he said wryly. "Can we start over?" He held out his hand and offered a lopsided, irresistibly appealing smile. "Hi, I'm Adam Case."

He waited, neither the smile nor his direct, slightly challenging gaze wavering, until she gave him her hand and murmured reluctantly, "Jenna Kendrick."

"Nice to meet you, Jenna Kendrick. I don't believe in wasting time or energy, so I'll tell you right now that I'd like to get to know you. Partly because I'm new in town and feelin' lonely as an orphaned hound dog, but mostly because you're the prettiest lady I've met in a coon's age and I've always had a special weakness for women with big, brown eyes."

She laughed, as of course he meant her to. Orphaned hound dog, indeed. At the same time, she couldn't help remembering that when he'd first presented himself at Verda's desk, he'd reminded her of a friendly puppy. His amiable, gently coaxing smile unexpectedly triggered a white-hot flare of rage toward Dennis Barnes: Why did he have to reenter her life *now,* just as the most handsome, charming man she'd ever met came along? Adam Case seemed too good to be true. Was he, literally? Did she dare let down her guard and seize the opportunity fate kept knocking her over the head with?

He claimed to have a weakness for women with big, brown eyes. As Jenna returned his calm, steady gaze, she discovered that she, too, had a few weaknesses she hadn't known about till now, including one for *men* with brown eyes...and dimples that played hide-and-seek, and thick dark hair that gleamed like sable in the sunlight. And drawls. Oh, yes, she definitely had a previously undiscovered weakness for deep, languorous, giddyap-li'l-doggie drawls.

"We'd better hurry," she said as she stood up, impatiently brushing sugar-cone crumbs from her skirt, "and pray there isn't a long line for tickets."

ADAM HADN'T ANTICIPATED having to work this hard. He'd figured she might be unresponsive at first, especially since she knew Barnes would be getting out soon. But he hadn't counted on having to overcome such determined resistance.

When he first saw her in the tavern, he'd known right away that she was nervous, uptight. She'd barely tasted the hash, and her eyes kept darting around, checking out the lunchtime crowd as if she expected...

What? At the time, he'd thought she might suspect she was being watched. And of course she was, by him. But in retrospect, it seemed her uneasiness had had an edge of fear. She'd been jumpy, tense... suspicious.

He'd seen the same suspicion at the agency, when she'd placed him from the tavern. A guarded, wary look had suddenly clouded those enormous, expressive eyes, and she'd sent out a chill that would have given a polar bear frostbite. Her reaction had momentarily thrown him. She couldn't have remembered him from the trial, could she? They'd never met, and when she was escorted to or from the courtroom, she'd always stared straight ahead, refusing to meet anyone's eyes except while she was on the stand, giving testimony.

No, he'd decided, she couldn't know who he was. Attributing her wariness to a criminal's instinctive caution, he launched his campaign to put her at ease. The first sign that he was having any success had been the laugh he surprised out of her with the remark about the tavern's greasy food. That spontaneous laugh had been a real jolt—rich and throaty, sexy as hell. It had rattled him for a moment, until he reminded himself who she was and why he was there.

He relaxed a little after that, believing he'd made some headway. But then she unaccountably retreated into the deep freeze when he asked her to lunch. It had been pure stubbornness that made him follow her to the riverfront, and maybe just a touch of offended pride. He'd been knocking himself out, and the results so far had been disappointing, to say the least.

He'd waited a while to be sure she wasn't meeting someone before he approached her, armed with a fresh determination to break through that glacial wall she was hiding behind and spurred by a compulsion to prove that he could. But an odd thing happened as he drew closer. The sight of her, sitting there under the blazing noontime sun, hugging her arms as if she were chilled to the bone, had brought him up short.

She'd looked lost . . . forlorn. Scared.

He had impatiently dismissed the impressions and the unwelcome twinge of concern that accompanied them. Of course she wasn't afraid; she had no reason to be. It had been an illusion, a trick of his mind. Gazing too long at that deceptively sweet, innocent face of hers could make a man imagine all sorts of foolish nonsense.

It had taken a bit more effort, but he'd finally started to get past her distrust. They'd ridden the small, cramped elevator to the top of the Arch, then spent an amicable ten minutes or so leaning over the small observation windows, staring down past their own feet and out across the river. The interlude had been a limited victory, because as soon as they were back on terra firma, she'd had to rush back to her job. But at least she was smiling when they parted company. He had one foot in the door. It was a good start.

So why did he feel so dissatisfied as he watched her drive away—as if his plan had already been derailed?

JENNA HADN'T FELT LIKE this in a very long time. Too long. She searched for a word to describe the unaccustomed lightness, the delicious warmth that seemed to be radiating from someplace deep inside her. The only one that came close was *carefree.*

It was a dangerous word, a dangerous *state,* especially now. She wasn't free of care—far from it. She knew she couldn't afford to let down her guard, even for a second. But it had felt so *good* to relax and just enjoy herself for those few precious minutes—it was like being let out of prison.

An appropriate analogy, she thought with a fresh surge of resentment. Dennis Barnes wasn't the only one who'd been in government custody for five years. The difference was that his incarceration was appropriate and just; he'd earned every minute of every day, and then some. Her only crime had been to tell the truth about what she knew.

She forced herself to swallow the bitterness that rose like bile whenever she started to brood about what her selfless act had cost her. It was over, done, ancient history. The here and now was what mattered, and that included calculating this month's sales commissions. Deliberately blotting out thoughts of Dennis Barnes, she focused on the stack of contracts in front of her.

She was almost finished when the door opened and a delivery boy wearing a tan-and-orange uniform breezed in. Verda was away from her desk, so he turned to Jenna, who was closest to the entrance, and announced, "Got a package for a Jenna Kendrick. She here?"

"Yes. I'm Jenna Kendrick."

She held out her hand for his clipboard and signed on the appropriate line. It didn't occur to her until the young man had gone that she wasn't expecting any deliveries. She stared at the parcel he'd deposited on her desk—a rectangular cardboard box, about the size and shape of a shoebox—and tried to subdue the panic that sprang up out of nowhere.

"What's that—a present?"

The question came from Liza Roper as she dropped a new contract on top of the stack Jenna had already worked her way through.

"I don't know," Jenna murmured. "It was just delivered."

"Well, aren't you going to open it?"

Good question. *Should* she open the box? What if it contained a bomb, or—and this possibility was equally terrifying—a simple, straightforward threat? Maybe she should call Roy Stevenson, let him decide how to deal with the package. That was part of his job, wasn't it, to evaluate any possible threats to her?

"It's not your birthday, is it?"

Apparently Liza wasn't going to return to her own desk until her curiosity had been satisfied. She picked up the box and shook it gently. Jenna's breath jammed in her throat.

"Doesn't rattle," Liza said with a frown. "It's too big to be jewelry, anyway. Oh, hey—maybe you won one of those sweepstakes!"

Jenna's hands trembled slightly as she reached out and relieved Liza of the box, resisting the urge to snatch it from her. "I never enter those things."

"Then it must be a present. From the guy who's been costing you sleep, I bet—a let's-kiss-and-make-up peace offering."

Verda Young appeared from the direction of the kitchenette, limping slowly on her bandaged foot. "What's in the box?"

"A present from Jen's beau," Liza replied.

Verda's salt-and-pepper eyebrows rose inquisitively above her bifocals. "I didn't know you had a beau."

"They had a lover's spat a few days ago," Liza confided. "But now he's come to his senses and wants to make up."

"Oh, that's nice," Verda said. She smiled expectantly.

Meanwhile, Liza's response to the exasperated look Jenna shot her was to fold her arms under her impressive bosom and grin. "I'm not budging till I see what it is."

Jenna couldn't think of an excuse or delaying tactic that wouldn't either offend the other women or make them suspicious... or do both. She opened a desk drawer and located a pair of scissors, telling herself it was ridiculous to be afraid of a cardboard box. Barnes wouldn't send a bomb to do her in. If he intended to kill her, and that was a definite possibility, he'd prefer to use his bare hands. And he'd drag it out as long as possible, savoring every moment.

A couple of quick snips dispensed with the strapping tape that secured the box. Jenna took a deep breath and carefully eased the flaps apart, then just as carefully lifted out a wad of robin's-egg-blue tissue paper. Verda and Liza leaned over the desk, eyes glittering with anticipation.

When the object beneath the paper was finally exposed, Verda murmured a soft, slightly bewildered "Oh, my." Liza expelled a sharp, surprised laugh. Neither of them could possibly have been as dumbfounded as Jenna.

Nestled on a bed of more tissue paper and gazing up at her with the most desolate brown eyes she'd ever seen was a plush basset hound—the kind little girls cuddle up with in bed. A round metal tag was attached to the red velvet ribbon around his neck. The name Adam was engraved on the tag.

Chapter Three

"There's a card," Liza pointed out.

So there was—the kind that folded twice and sealed to form its own envelope. Jenna pulled it from the box, glancing briefly at the bold black script that spelled out her name, while Liza plucked the stuffed toy from its tissue-paper bed.

"Isn't it precious!" she crooned. "So his name's Adam, huh?"

Jenna nodded, not stopping to consider that she might be encouraging Liza's speculation. Inside the folded card was a short note:

> He's housebroken and low-maintenance. (So am
> I, by the way.) You're a terrific tour guide. How
> about a moonlight cruise next?

The signature was a simple "Adam," but he'd added a local phone number below his name. Not too subtle, Jenna thought wryly.

"Adam what?" Verda asked. "What's he do for a living?"

Liza nudged her with an elbow. "Don't be so nosy."

The older woman gave an affronted snort. "Look who's talking. Besides, I don't think it's being nosy to show a little friendly concern. There are a lot of perverts prowling around nowadays."

"No pervert could get within a mile of Jen," Liza retorted. "She's too sharp."

Verda pursed her lips and shook her head in a way that managed to express both skepticism and maternal anxiety, then limped off to her own desk. As soon as she was out of earshot, Liza set the basset hound on Jenna's blotter and leaned close to murmur, "All right, give. Who is he? Where'd you meet him? What's he look like?"

Jenna reached out to stroke the soft, plush fabric with an index finger. Her lips curved in an involuntary smile. There *was* a slight resemblance in the eyes....

"He's tall—about six-two, I guess—and slim. Dark brown hair, brown eyes. He's a free-lance writer." She trailed off and shrugged. "That's all I know, really. I only met him this morning, when he came in to buy a renter's policy."

"You just met him today?"

A sudden sharpness in Liza's voice caused Jenna to glance up in surprise. "Yes, like I said, he came in to ask about renter's insurance while you were out showing the Marcus Avenue listing. Why?"

Liza shook her head. "Nothing. I just assumed he must be the man who's been costing you sleep. Guess that was some other guy, huh?"

Jenna had forgotten Liza's probing the previous morning, and her impulsive, careless response. She shifted her attention back to the dog, aware that the reminder of Dennis Barnes had caused her expression to harden.

"Yes," she confirmed quietly. "That was somebody else."

Liza straightened and smoothed her short linen skirt, her curiosity apparently satisfied for the moment. "Well, this Adam seems like a good prospect. Any man who'd send you a stuffed toy when he's known you less than twenty-four hours has to be a hopeless romantic."

"You think so?" Jenna murmured.

"I *know* so, honey. Take my advice and snatch him up before somebody else does."

The advice kept replaying on Jenna's mental tape recorder all afternoon. Of course Liza was right—if circumstances had been different, she'd have thanked her lucky stars that Adam Case had picked this agency to stroll into. But her life was a big enough mess right now. She didn't need any new complications. She didn't *want* a personal involvement that would only make things more difficult.

And if those weren't good enough reasons to resist his undeniable appeal, there was the nagging uncertainty that hovered like a dark cloud at the edge of her consciousness: was he really who and what he claimed to be? Could his appearance—here, this week—be as coincidental as it seemed?

THE OWNER OF THE SECURITY firm whose ad she'd picked out of the yellow pages had been apologetic, but adamant that he wouldn't be able to install the system Jenna wanted until the following week. Suburban crime rates were up, he'd explained over the phone this morning, before she left for work. Property owners were increasingly nervous. Business was booming and his technicians were all working overtime.

When Jenna made the point that she was a woman living alone, he'd offered to send someone to her house that evening to set up a temporary alarm system. It wouldn't be fancy or high tech, he said, but if anybody tried to force his way past the lock on her front door, the siren should send him running for cover. Of course, if she or any close neighbors had pets, they'd probably make quite a fuss, not to mention a mess on the carpet.

Jenna had accepted the offer without a second's hesitation or a single qualm about the hyperactive Chihuahua across the street.

A plain, dark blue van was parked at the curb in front of her house when she pulled into the drive at a quarter past five. A tall young man in a crisp blue-and-gray uniform got out, then waited on the sidewalk, letting her approach him. Jenna liked that.

"Ms. Kendrick?" he said in a brisk, no-nonsense tone.

She nodded. "Yes."

A clip-on laminated badge was fastened to his shirt pocket. The badge bore the name, address and phone number of the security company, a color photo of the man facing her and, beneath the photo, the name Marvin Bolander. Jenna felt safer already. These people were obviously professionals.

"Are you here to install the alarm?"

"Yes, ma'am. But first I'll need to see some identification, to verify that this is your residence."

When she got over her surprise, she dug out her wallet and handed it to him, then waited while he compared her face with the photo on her driver's license and scanned the few credit cards she possessed to make sure the same name was on everything. Her feeling of security increased; this guy sure took his job seriously.

In under twenty minutes, he had installed the alarm and explained how it worked. Then he stepped onto the small front porch, had Jenna lock the door from inside and tried to jimmy it with a flat-blade screwdriver. Even though she was expecting a loud noise, she nearly jumped out of her shoes when the speaker he'd fastened to the exterior wall, directly above the door, suddenly discharged a deafening high-pitched screech. The sound bored right through aluminum siding, insulation and drywall and jabbed red-hot needles into her eardrums. Grimacing, she lunged for the switch next to the door to deactivate the alarm, then unlocked the door and yanked it open.

"Lord, Marvin! Does this thing have a volume control?"

He grinned and shook his head. "There's one setting—wake-the-dead."

Jenna grimaced again and massaged her ears. They were still ringing. Across the street, poor Pepe was probably dangling from his owner's chandelier.

"I'll be back next Friday to install the complete system you ordered," Marvin told her as he replaced the screwdriver in his toolbox. "Five-thirty be okay?"

"That'll be fine," she agreed.

After Marvin climbed into his van and drove off, she relocked the door, reset the alarm and went to the kitchen to find something to eat. Should she notify Roy Stevenson about the precaution she'd taken? No, she decided as she contemplated a selection of frozen dinners. He would only recite the standard spiel—she shouldn't worry, the Marshals Service was on top of the situation, Dennis Barnes couldn't possibly know where she was or what name she was using. Et cetera, et cetera.

And they'd both know it was all so much Justice Department flimflam.

She couldn't hold it against him, though. He'd been trained—or maybe *programmed* was a better word—by the United States government, after all. Enormous amounts of taxpayers' money had been invested to produce a company man, a team player. And Uncle Roy was certainly a company man, to the toes of his generic black cotton-blend socks. He had the official line down cold, and he never wavered from it.

She'd just taken a chicken fettucine dinner out of the microwave when the phone rang. Expecting it to be either Roy or someone from the agency, she was startled when Adam Case's drawl caressed her recently abused ear.

"Did I catch you at suppertime?"

"As a matter of fact, you did." Surprise and instinctive wariness made her sound a little brusque. "How did you get my number?"

If he noticed the edge in her voice, it didn't seem to bother him. "Dialed directory assistance, gave the guy who answered your name. I wish the phone companies would go back to only hiring women operators. These young studs always sound like they're trolling, know what I mean? Makes me nervous as hell."

Jenna was glad he couldn't see her smile. "Careful, your prejudices are showing."

"Well, I'm a Texan, born and bred," he replied. His wry tone made it both an explanation and a defense, but definitely not an apology.

She closed her eyes and leaned back against the wall. No doubt about it, Mr. Case was a seductively tantalizing package—rugged good looks, irresistible charm and an often unsettling candor. It was that unregenerate, take-it-or-leave-it directness that might be her undoing. It had been a long time since she'd met a man with the confidence and integrity to just be himself.

"Thanks for Adam, Jr.," she murmured. "He's adorable."

"So's Adam, Sr., once you get to know him."

It was such a brazen come-on that Jenna rolled her eyes in response. He *had* warned her that he didn't believe in wasting time or energy. She smiled again, something she hadn't done much lately, until a certain lean, tall Texan had sauntered into her life. She could very easily make it a habit.

"What exactly did you have in mind?" she heard herself ask, and experienced a small jolt of surprise. *Watch it!* her practical, calculating self counseled. *You know next to nothing about this man.*

But then something strange happened. Her intuitive, impulsive self abruptly decided to take control— probably because after five years it was fed up with being muzzled—and cheerfully disregarded the warning. So that when his deep, sexy-as-sin response poured into her ear, her knees actually quivered and her heart went crazy for several wild, impetuous beats.

"Well, now, I was hopin' you'd ask."

THEY SPENT HER LUNCH hour on Thursday wandering around the zoo, eating chili dogs and Sno-Kones and tossing prepackaged food they got from vending machines to the animals. Jenna was ten minutes late getting back to the office, an offense she'd never committed before but for which she felt not the slightest twinge of guilt. Adam wanted to take her to an Aerosmith concert that night. She declined, claiming she'd promised to go to the movies with a friend, then spent the evening watching a series of Katharine Hepburn movies on cable and wishing she'd said yes to the concert. Only partly because she loved Aerosmith.

The effervescent warmth buzzing through her veins had her worried. So did her uncharacteristic lack of caution. When she was with Adam, she forgot to be alert, on guard. She forgot that she couldn't just relax, let her hair down and have a good time. He was so easy to be with, to talk to, that she'd responded to him like a tightly closed bud suddenly exposed to the heat and light of the sun. She'd been aware that it was happening, even a little concerned, yet she hadn't done a thing to stop it.

That was what troubled her most—the knowledge that she'd been conscious of her own actions and reactions every minute she was with him. It was as if she'd split into two people: the spectator and the participant. The Jenna who watched knew that the other Jenna could have pulled back into herself, withdrawn behind the cool, distant facade, at any time. She hadn't. She'd *chosen* not to shut Adam out.

The reason was transparently obvious. She'd been happy while she was with him—genuinely happy, for the first time in five years. She hadn't wanted the interlude to end. It was Adam who eventually noticed the time and hurried her back to his car, a '66 Mustang almost as old as Jenna.

At midnight she turned off the television and reluctantly went to bed. But for the first time that week Dennis Barnes wasn't waiting to pursue her down endless dark, dangerous corridors. Instead, in her dreams she strolled along the riverfront, delighting in the sounds of children playing, and basking in brilliant August sunshine...and in the warmth of a slow, sensual smile.

The delivery of a five-pound box of Godiva chocolates the following afternoon caused quite a stir among Jenna's co-workers. Liza, Verda and Ellie Dyson crowded around her desk to ooh and ahh, sample the candy, and inspect the accompanying small, square card that bore only a large, perfectly centered *A*. After the trio returned to their own desks, Jenna tried to concentrate on updating the current real estate listings, hoping the task would take her mind off the fluttery sensation directly beneath her breastbone. The strategy wasn't working worth a damn, so she welcomed the distraction when the phone on her desk rang.

"I think it's him," Verda's excited voice announced over the intercom. She spoke in a stage whisper, as if she was afraid the caller she'd put on hold might overhear. "You know—*him! Adam!* On line two."

Jenna murmured a quiet thanks and disconnected Verda's line, then inhaled a deep breath and released it slowly. She stared at the blinking button for line two. Okay. Time to get serious, nip this thing in the bud. There was no way she could become involved with Adam Case. She *couldn't,* and that was all there was to it. The longer she put off making that clear—to herself, as well as to him—the more complicated things would get.

"Is your sweet tooth satisfied?" he asked as soon as she identified herself.

His voice was even more potent over the phone, as if being digitized and sent zinging through miles of fiber optics had somehow distilled it to the essence of male sexuality. Jenna closed her eyes and tried to dredge up some willpower.

"Travel writing must pay well," she observed, avoiding a direct answer and the requisite thank-you. Better he should think her rude than risk letting him completely demolish her resolve, which, heaven knew, wasn't unshakable to begin with. Keeping her tone impassive required a substantial effort, but the slight pause before Adam's reply told her he'd noticed.

"I live simply, and I don't have a family to support."

His drawl was still honey-smooth, but it contained a shade less overt sensuality. It was an indication of Jenna's emotional turmoil that she couldn't decide whether she was gratified or disappointed.

"What's the matter? Get up on the wrong side of bed this morning, or did I call at a bad time?" he asked with the frankness she'd already come to expect from him.

He'd given her a perfect opening. All she had to do was let him know, tactfully but firmly, that she wasn't interested. *Do it,* she told herself. *Now, before you lose your nerve.*

Too late. A tight, panicky feeling suddenly squeezed her chest. Her entire body tensed, her pulse and respiration accelerating dramatically. Jenna recognized the fight-or-flight response and thought she understood the reason for it: on some very basic level she felt threatened or, more likely, provoked. By the thought of rejecting Adam, apparently, and the unexpected pleasure he'd brought into her life.

She hesitated for a crucial moment and her gaze lit on the typed list of properties in front of her.

"As a matter of fact, I am pretty busy."

Stop stalling. Do it!

"I won't keep you, then," Adam said. She thought he sounded relieved. Her heart gave an excited little leap. "I just wanted to—"

Jenna heard a distinct click on the line. "Excuse me," she interrupted. Then, to whoever had picked up one of the other phones, "This line is in use."

A female voice muttered, "Oh, sorry!" and there was another click. Jenna wasn't able to identify the woman. It might have been Liza, Ellie or even Verda, though that seemed unlikely since Verda's desk was in her direct line of sight, while the other two were behind her. At the moment Verda was on the phone, but she could have been in the middle of a conversation or have just answered an incoming call.

Adam's lazy drawl reclaimed her attention. "As I was about to say, I called to ask you to dinner."

Jenna's grip tightened on the receiver. "Dinner?"

No! Just give it to him straight—no dinner, no concerts, no moonlight cruises. Not tonight, not any other night.

She opened her mouth, then closed it again without uttering a sound. She suddenly felt as if she were poised on the rim of a steep precipice, and the slightest movement would upset her balance, pitching her forward into the unknown, or backward to solid ground and safety.

"Dinner," he repeated with exaggerated patience. "You know, the meal you have late in the day, between lunch and a midnight snack. I can see we need to work on your vocabulary."

His wry humor was the equivalent of a gentle nudge between her shoulder blades. Not giving herself time to reconsider, Jenna took a deep, fortifying breath and then a giant mental step forward.

"I'd like to have dinner with you, Adam."

She realized as she spoke the words that this wasn't a whim she would regret as soon as she hung up the phone. There would be no reneging, no going back. The knowledge was frightening, but at the same time strangely exhilarating. Liberating. Whatever might be waiting at the bottom of the cliff she'd just hurled herself from, the fall wasn't likely to kill her. And she'd known for some time that safety and security were illusions, lies people bought into to keep from going stark raving mad.

Besides, she trusted this man. She couldn't think of a single reason why she should, but she did. His blunt, unabashed honesty had already begun to chip away at the cynicism and distrust that had encased her like armor for the past five years. It also made him the only person in her life, including Roy Stevenson, whom she *did* trust at the moment. Adam had no hidden agendas. To him, she was a woman, not a pawn.

"Great! How about if I pick you up at the office," he suggested. "We might want to grab an early meal and then take in a movie, or maybe check out one of those cruises."

A moonlight cruise on the Mississippi. The warmth he'd kindled spread until it suffused her whole body. "Sounds good to me," she murmured. "I get off at five."

SIX DAYS. THAT'S ALL he had; less, if Barnes was released the day of his hearing. Adam doubted it would be enough time.

He collected the reports he'd been reviewing, replaced them in Dennis Barnes's file and locked the file in the bottom drawer of his rented desk. He could have used another week; two would be even better. The thaw had started, but it was a frustratingly slow process. He didn't dare press Jenna about her background yet, much less try to find out about any future plans. He'd got the message loud and clear last night, standing on the top deck of a stern-wheeler making its lazy way upriver: certain topics were strictly off-limits.

His first attempt to draw her out had been innocuous enough. He'd asked how long she'd lived in St. Louis. It was the kind of question anyone might ask a new acquaintance. She should have expected it—at any rate, shouldn't have been thrown by it—but her discomfort had been obvious. First her eyes clouded over—those lovely, gold-flecked eyes that could easily entice a man to his own ruin, if he wasn't aware of the cunning that lay behind them. Then she ducked her head and turned away slightly, tension radiating from her in waves as she gave a terse reply and quickly changed the subject.

Her response had been the same to casual questions about her family, which wasn't really surprising. Adam knew about her sister and nephew, that Kayla Barnes had been leaving her husband when the plane she and their only child were aboard crashed. He understood the pain that being reminded of the tragedy must cause Jenna. He even found himself sympathizing, despite his belief that her relationship with Barnes had been more than employer-employee and brother- and sister-in-law.

His own compassion had surprised and unsettled him, but her continued reticence troubled him more, made him uneasy in ways he couldn't define. At first he'd chalked her hands-off attitude up to the paranoia most lawbreakers exhibit at some point. But the more time he spent with her, the less faith he had in that initial presumption. His gut instinct told him the reasons for her restraint went deeper than that.

The woman was an enigma. She tensed up like a terrified virgin at his most casual touch, which, given what he knew about her background, was baffling. She'd been twenty-four when she testified at Barnes's trial, which would make her almost thirty now. But a couple of times last night—when she leaned over the rail to watch the huge paddle wheel churn the river to a tan froth, and again when the calliope warmed up with a series of agonized shrieks—she hadn't looked a day over twenty.

Adam deliberately blocked the memory of her spontaneous, startlingly sensual laughter and the effect it had had on him. For those few moments he'd forgotten who they were, why he was with her. A lapse he vowed grimly not to repeat. He had five days—six, tops. He didn't intend to waste a minute of that time.

AT THREE MINUTES to five, the door of Pendergrass and Son opened and a huge bouquet of flowers walked in. At least, at first it looked like a walking bouquet. The loosely bundled flowers and accompanying foliage practically filled the narrow doorway, and a pair of legs stuck out at the bottom.

Long legs clad in snug blue denim jeans, Jenna realized as the sheaf rotated slowly in her direction. Beneath the jeans was a pair of tobacco-brown cowboy boots.

The colorful vegetation spoke.

"I hope to goodness you don't have hay fever."

Chapter Four

There wasn't room in Adam's Mustang for the two of them and the flowers, so Jenna stuck the bouquet in a plastic wastebasket Verda unearthed in the storage room, added several cups of water and left it on her desk.

First they had dinner at a Mexican restaurant, then took in the film at the theater that had been carved out of the bedrock beneath the Arch, and wound up the evening at a suburban skating rink. Jenna didn't comment on Adam's apparently impulsive choices. She'd decided as soon as she recognized his jeans and boots to sit back and enjoy the ride. And she did, enormously, even though she hadn't laced on a pair of roller skates since she was twelve years old. Fortunately Adam stayed glued to her side, his arm around her waist to keep her from careening into the walls or other skaters.

Only later, after they'd returned to the agency to collect the king-size bouquet and her car, did it occur to her that maybe taking her skating hadn't been such an impulsive decision after all. It *had* provided the perfect excuse for almost constant physical contact, but a respectable, nonthreatening contact, in a well-lit, public place. Had he considered those things in advance? she wondered as she drove past him on her way out of the small parking lot.

She glanced at the rearview mirror in time to see him duck into his car. He'd waited until she was safely locked inside hers and on her way.

Jenna shook her head with a quizzical smile. His old-fashioned chivalry continued to surprise her. She'd spent the ride from the skating rink worrying about how she should react if he made a pass, and then he hadn't even tried for a good-night kiss. Her relief had almost equaled her disappointment—didn't he *want* to kiss her?—until the mortifying possibility occurred to her that he might be afraid she'd scream or faint or knee him in the groin.

She was painfully aware that she wouldn't have won the Miss Congeniality award tonight. Face it, she concluded glumly during the twenty-minute drive home, a slug would have been a more exciting date, and probably a better conversationalist.

Yet she was also aware that Adam had been patiently and diligently trying to draw her out, to get her to loosen up. Heaven knew why he bothered. No man with his combination of drop-dead looks and lethal charm would lack for female companionship unless it was by choice. She was fairly sure that Liza Roper, for instance, would jump at the chance to spend an evening with Adam Case—the entire evening, right through to sunup. Liza had almost tripped over her own tongue when he came out from behind the flowers and she got her first look at him.

By the time Jenna pulled into her drive, she was feeling depressed, dissatisfied with herself and life in general, and resentful of the Liza Ropers of the world, whose biggest problem was deciding what shade of eyeshadow to put on in the morning. She lugged the flowers Adam had brought her to the porch and balanced the wastebasket on her hip to unlock the door. The wastebasket slipped, dribbling water down the left side of her skirt. She swore under her breath.

"Looks like you could use some help."

The amused remark wafted out of the darkness behind her. She jumped and more water sloshed onto her thigh. A second later a pair of lean brown hands relieved her of the makeshift vase. Jenna whirled around and stared at Adam, her heart in her throat.

He held the wastebasket at arm's length. A rueful smile exposed the dimple in his right cheek. "Next time I think I'll settle for a single long-stemmed rose."

"You followed me home."

She knew it sounded like an accusation, but at the moment she was too unstrung to have much control over the tone of her voice. *Why* had he followed her? And why hadn't she been aware that he was? Dear God, he could have been anybody—a burglar, some punk out to hijack her car...

Somebody sent by Dennis Barnes.

An icy chill swept over her. She'd been so busy feeling sorry for herself that she hadn't paid the slightest attention to the traffic around her. She didn't even remember turning off Manchester, or onto her own street, for that matter.

"It's late," Adam said by way of explanation. "I just thought..." He trailed off with a shrug and a sheepish smile. "Go ahead, write me off as a dyed-in-the-wool chauvinist. I can't help it."

He'd followed her to be sure she made it home all right! Jenna didn't know what to say. Flustered and embarrassed and wanting to hide the guilt she knew had colored her face, she concentrated on unlocking the door. This was what living with suspicion and distrust day after day, year after year, did to you. You ended up questioning the motives and intentions of everyone you met...even somebody as relentlessly straight-arrow as Adam Case.

She opened the door, then impulsively turned and gave him a self-conscious smile. "Actually, I think it was sweet of you to be concerned. Can I offer you a cold drink to show my appreciation?"

Adam accepted the invitation and followed her inside. The second Jenna closed the door behind them, her nervous tension zoomed to an all-time high. Until now, Roy Stevenson was the only man who'd entered the house during the five years she'd occupied it who hadn't been summoned to install or repair something. She wasn't at all sure she was up to playing hostess, especially to this man.

"The kitchen's through here," she murmured, turning to lead the way.

"Is that where you want the portable rain forest?"

She glanced over her shoulder and saw that the wastebasket had sprung a leak and was leaving a trail of water on the carpet. Wonderful. More stress she didn't need.

"I guess. Either there or the bathroom."

"Why don't I just stick it in the tub for now," he suggested.

Jenna nodded in relief. "Good idea. It's the second door on the right."

As soon as he was headed down the hall, she hurried into the kitchen, switched on the light and grabbed a dishtowel to blot her sodden skirt. A quick glance around convinced her that asking him in had been a mistake. Her breakfast dishes were piled in the sink, it had been at least a month since she mopped the floor, and she probably looked like the "Before" picture in one of those head-to-toe makeover ads.

"Talk about feelin' like a grade-A fool," Adam drawled as he sauntered into the room. Jenna glanced up with a startled, questioning frown. "The flowers," he explained. "I'll replace your skirt."

"Oh...no!" she blurted, then flung the towel onto the counter as if she'd been caught in possession of incriminating evidence at the scene of a crime. "Really, that isn't necessary. It's only water."

For a moment she thought he would insist, but then his rugged features relaxed into one of the boyish, lopsided smiles that played havoc with her pulse rate. "Okay. This is a nice house. Cozy. It fits you."

The observation was another small shock. He thought *cozy* fit her?

"Thanks," she murmured. "I like it."

He leaned against a cabinet and watched while she opened the refrigerator and removed a bottle of apple juice in one hand and a pitcher of orange juice in the other.

Adam took the apple juice from her with a quiet "Thanks."

His tone was subdued, his expression disconcertingly intent. Glad for an excuse to avoid his dark, piercing gaze, she opened an upper cabinet to collect two glasses.

"Jenna."

"Hmmm?" She kept her gaze averted, setting the glasses on the counter, pouring orange juice into one.

"I'm sorry."

Her head jerked up and around. A few drops of juice splattered on the Formica counter.

"What?"

"I said I'm sorry." Adam placed the bottle of apple juice on the counter and ripped a paper towel from the roll hanging next to the sink. "That you didn't enjoy yourself tonight," he added as he wiped the counter.

"But . . . no, I—"

He lifted a hand to forestall her protest and tossed the paper towel into the wastebasket. "It's okay. You don't have to fib to make me feel better. My ego's healthy enough to survive a little rejection now and then."

Rejection! The notion was so absurd that Jenna almost laughed. "I'm not," she stammered. "I wouldn't. Adam, I had a wonderful time. A *terrific* time!"

He didn't reply; didn't react at all, in fact. Except for a small vertical crease that had appeared between his eyebrows, his expression was an inscrutable mask. Did that little wrinkle mean he didn't believe her?

"I'm the one who should apologize," she said huskily. "I realize I'm not the world's most exciting date." For roughly half a second she considered telling him the whole, unvarnished truth, but her courage fled at the thought. She ducked her head and muttered, "I've always been a little . . . inhibited. . . ."

Especially the past five years. You see, there's this psychopath I sent to prison . . .

"I'm afraid I'm not very good in social situations."

Several seconds dragged by in nerve-racking silence. And then Adam slipped his fingers under her chin and gently tipped up her head. "Are you telling me you're shy?"

His expression hadn't changed, but he sounded surprised. Even incredulous. Jenna moved her shoulders in an embarrassed shrug but otherwise stood perfectly still, determined not to squirm.

"Well, now," he murmured at length. "We'll have to work on that."

His voice was deep and rich, sexy as hell. A tingling warmth began where he touched her and quickly spread throughout Jenna's body as she looked into his glittering eyes. She could have sworn they'd been cool and distant a moment ago, but obviously she'd been mistaken. There was nothing cool about this man.

It was suddenly hard to breathe, as if all the oxygen had been sucked out of the room. Her skin felt flushed and prickly, hypersensitive. In fact, all her senses had sharpened. The acid tang of orange juice stung her nose, and the hum of the refrigerator's condenser sounded like a freight train in the brittle silence as she met his smoldering gaze, unable to look away.

Her heart thudded in distress. She wasn't ready for this, had no idea what was supposed to happen next. She tried to think of a clever remark to break the tension, but at that moment she couldn't have strung five words together if someone had held a gun to her head.

Fortunately Adam's inherent chivalry and infallible timing saved her from making a fool of herself. He withdrew his hand slowly, rubbing his thumb across her chin in passing, then turned to pour himself a couple of ounces of apple juice—just enough to down in a single gulp. Jenna folded her arms tightly under her breasts. That abrupt, restless gesture said a lot about his emotional state, which apparently wasn't in much better shape than her own. She instinctively knew he was wishing the apple juice was something stronger.

"I think I'd better be going," he said.

And then he kissed her.

It was a light, brief kiss, but it made Jenna feel as if she'd stepped on a high-tension electrical cable.

"—okay?"

She blinked to bring his face into focus. There was a weird fizzing in her ears, as if she'd stuck her head into a bucket of champagne. "I'm sorry. What?"

"I said I'll call you in the morning, if that's all right."

Jenna nodded. She thought she murmured, "Okay," though she couldn't be sure. She walked him to the door, closed and locked it behind him, switched on the alarm, then slowly raised her fingers to her mouth. Her lips were still tingling. It was a good thing he hadn't kissed her again before he left, she thought giddily. She might have passed out cold.

When she heard his car pull away from the curb, she leaned back against the solid oak door and closed her eyes. Two things had become shockingly clear in the last few minutes. One, she wasn't the only one who had been grappling with self-imposed restraints. Adam had been holding back, too. *Had been*—past tense. And, two, he wanted a lot more from her than a transitory, no-strings relationship.

She knew without even thinking about it that Adam Case usually got what he wanted.

She was in deep, deep trouble.

HE WAS IN TROUBLE.

He'd completely lost his objectivity tonight, started relating to her as a living, breathing person, instead of simply the means to an end. Truth time, his conscience sniped as he reached for a towel and stepped out of the shower. He'd seen her not just as a person, but as a woman—a beautiful, desirable, unexpectedly vulnerable woman.

The physical attraction was an unwelcome distraction, but he could deal with it, keep it under control. It was her vulnerability that had knocked him off course and was still threatening to undermine his resolve. She couldn't be that good an actress, could she? Her anxiety when she realized he'd followed her had been real; as real as the poignant self-consciousness that had blasted all his comfortable assumptions about her to smithereens.

He stood in front of the mirror over the washbasin, glaring at his reflection until he'd managed to purge himself of sentiment and restore his sense of purpose. Hell, yes, she was an accomplished actress! She'd been good enough to convince the attorney general's staff she was only doing her patriotic duty when she'd volunteered to testify against Dennis Barnes. She'd apparently convinced Roy Stevenson, as well, and Roy was no pushover.

"Neither am I," he promised himself in a grim tone as he switched off the bathroom light. Starting first thing tomorrow, he intended to monopolize every available second of Jenna Kendrick's time. He had five days left to find out what she knew about Barnes's plans. He had to make every minute count.

BY TUESDAY EVENING, Jenna was seesawing wildly between light-headed euphoria and hopeless despair. Standing in front of the dresser mirror to remove her makeup, she was forced to acknowledge that the volatile emotional shifts were taking their toll, physically as well as emotionally. The proof was right there in front of her, in the fine lines around her mouth and the haunted look in her eyes.

She'd spent virtually every free minute of the past four days with Adam—a persistent, attentive, wonderfully romantic Adam, who had let her know in a dozen subtle and not-so-subtle ways that he was nuts about her and hell-bent on making her fall head over heels, out of her gourd in love with him.

She was very much afraid she already had.

She would have been a hundred percent sure, if not for the vulnerable periods very early in the morning and late at night, when she lay awake agonizing about whether her feelings for him were the real thing or just the predictable response of a woman who'd been starved for warmth and affection for five lonely years.

The doubt usually lasted no more than a few minutes before it was routed by defiant optimism: She *knew* what she felt was real, and that she would feel exactly the same way a year from now, or in five years, or twenty. The knowledge buoyed her throughout the day and the evenings they spent together... until she was alone in the dark again, with only self-doubt and guilty secrets for company.

And the guilt was ten times worse than the doubt. She couldn't go on like this. She had to bring this emotional roller-coaster ride to an end, and soon, for both their sakes. Adam Case was the most honest, forthright man she'd ever known. He deserved to know the truth—all of it, every sordid detail. By keeping it from him, she was intentionally lying. She hated that, hated the way it made her feel. Almost as much as she hated the thought of how he would react when she told him.

He might take off like a shot. She knew she had to accept that possibility. He was a decent, honorable man. Learning that she'd once been associated with someone like Dennis Barnes might destroy whatever he felt for her. But she had to take that chance. She couldn't even consider a future with Adam so long as her life was an elaborate, grotesque web of deceit.

She had tomorrow to prepare and try to brace herself for the worst. Adam was going out of town to do some research for one of his travel articles. He'd promised to call as soon as he got back, probably late in the afternoon. She would invite him to dinner, Jenna decided as she climbed into bed. They'd have a nice meal, some wine, and then when he was relaxed and comfortable, she'd set him down in the privacy of her "cozy" living room and tell him everything. She could do it. She *would* do it. She just wouldn't let herself think about the possible consequences.

TWO GUARDS CAME TO ESCORT Dennis Barnes to his parole hearing at ten minutes to ten on Wednesday morning. He walked between and slightly in front of them, relaxed and confident. When they reached the corridor that led to the hearing room, he directed an occasional brusque nod to one of the people waiting to address the board on his behalf. More than a dozen men, all well-known and respected in the arenas of banking and commerce, lined the corridor. Barnes acknowledged fewer than a third of them, aware that the others were mentally filing their names for future reference.

His shirt and trousers were new, and pressed to a starched crispness that made the guards' uniforms look shabby in comparison. The leather of his freshly polished shoes gleamed like black glass under the bare fluorescent bulbs. A sharp appearance was essential this morning—not for the parole board, but for the men in the corridor. Perception was everything. If he was seen to have lost ground during the last five years, the well-groomed piranhas in the thousand-dollar suits would have him stripped to the bone before he could relish his first breath of freedom.

That was why they were here. He wanted them to see for themselves that the man responsible for their success and prosperity hadn't changed, that his power was undiminished. Of course he needed a few of them, but only to lend credibility to the proceedings; the outcome of this hearing had been decided weeks ago.

A cold, sardonic smile flickered across his mouth when they reached the hearing room and he took a seat next to Everett Whitledge. It was the only display of emotion he would allow until the hearing was concluded. He separated himself from the drama unfolding around him, only partially attentive to the succession of appeals and testimonials. The next few hours were already history. His thoughts concerned the future. Specifically, what was going to happen in St. Louis tomorrow, or the day after....

ADAM SAT SLUMPED over the desk in his cramped studio apartment, glowering at the telephone as if it were to blame for the mess he was in.

The past four days had provided several major revelations, but from a professional standpoint they'd been a bust—"a waste of time and resources," as Roy Stevenson had predicted.

And that wasn't all Roy had been right about. Every stupid, arrogant assumption Adam had made concerning Jenna Kendrick had been wrong. The scheming opportunist he'd expected to find didn't exist; he was convinced now that she never had. She would be devastated when she found out how he'd used and deceived her, and why. She'd probably never forgive him. He wasn't sure he'd ever forgive himself.

Those had been hard truths to accept, but they couldn't compare to the final, mind-blowing Truth with a capital *T* that had been waiting to ambush him after he'd come to terms with his guilt and regret.

God help him, he'd fallen in love with her.

And she was going to hate him.

Adam reached for the phone, intending to check in with Roy, but found himself dialing the Pendergrass agency number instead. The receptionist answered on the second ring and for a moment he panicked. What the hell was he doing? He was supposed to be out of town all day.

"Hi, Verda," he heard himself say. "This is Adam Case. Is Jenna busy?"

The middle-aged woman coyly replied that Jenna was never too busy to talk to him and transferred the call at once. Guilt sliced through him in the seconds before she came on the line.

"Did you cancel your trip?" she asked. He thought she sounded anxious, rather than hopeful.

"No. I was thinking of you, so I decided to call and say hi."

There was a beat of static silence before she murmured a tepid "That's sweet."

Adam frowned. Something was wrong here.

"Is everything okay? You sound tired." *Or worried.*

"I'm fine. Just overworked, as usual. Listen, I was thinking—since you'll be on the road all day, why don't we stay in tonight? I'll cook. Is Italian okay?"

It sounded like a prepared speech. Adam's frown deepened, but he accepted the invitation and they agreed on seven-thirty. After he hung up, he stayed at the desk, replaying the brief conversation in his mind and trying to read between the lines. Had he imagined her reticence? Maybe someone had been standing there, listening, and what had sounded like reserve was only embarrassment or self-consciousness....

A random thought suddenly swooped out of nowhere, cutting short his theorizing. Among the information he'd received from Washington that morning had been a piece of news from one of Justice's prison informants. According to the informant, Dennis

Barnes's attorney had recently relayed several messages to a woman in St. Louis who was assisting Barnes with some "old business."

A *woman* in St. Louis.

Adam ruthlessly crushed the idea before it could burgeon into speculation. No. It wasn't possible. His judgment couldn't be that faulty.

You've sung that tune before, a small voice jeered. *It was your theme song for five years. How can you be sure you're right* this *time?*

Scrubbing a hand over his face, he reluctantly accepted that he couldn't be sure of anything where Jenna was concerned. He'd forfeited any claim to professional objectivity days ago—the first time he'd looked into those gold-flecked eyes, heard that husky laugh. He reached for the phone again. Roy Stevenson would have to sort it all out, come up with conclusions and recommendations. Roy was good at that kind of thing.

He'd punched out the first three digits of Roy's number when he remembered that Dennis Barnes's parole hearing was to take place today.

Chapter Five

Adam, Jr., watched from the center of Jenna's bed, his sorrowful eyes following her movements as she dressed.

She wished the basset hound could talk. She could have used some impartial advice—and not only about whether to wear the white cotton blouse or the apricot crepe de chine. She finally settled on the cotton, figuring it would be easier to clean or cheaper to replace if she threw up or spilled an entire glass of wine.

It was only six-twenty and she was already a basket case. She'd tried rehearsing how to tell Adam what she had to tell him, but that made her so self-conscious that everything came out hopelessly garbled. Next she tried memorizing notes she'd jotted down on index cards. The cards ended up at the bottom of the bathroom wastebasket.

"Get a grip, for pity's sake," she exhorted her wan reflection in the dresser mirror. "You can do this. It's *Adam* you'll be facing, not a firing squad or a gang of Justice Department androids."

She applied a little more peach blush, squared her shoulders and turned for the door. Time to put the lasagna in the oven. But as she was about to step into the hall, she impulsively stopped and looked back at Adam, Jr.

"Wish me luck," she whispered.

ADAM HAD NEVER BEEN this unsure of himself, of his instincts and judgment. His feelings for Jenna were smothering the first and distorting the second, so that it was impossible to form reliable conclusions based on the available information—including the just-received word that Barnes had been granted immediate parole shortly after noon today.

Was Jenna the contact Barnes had been sending messages to? His head said probably; his heart violently disagreed.

If his head was right, she could be planning to join Barnes in the next couple of days. But if his heart was right, Barnes may have been making arrangements to come after her... for revenge.

A succession of images and memories paraded through his mind: Sunday afternoon, when she'd realized that a hot-dog vendor had given him too much change and insisted on going back to return the extra money. Not the act of a dishonest woman. That brand new alarm at her front door. Why install an alarm, if she was planning to leave? Her anxiety the first time he'd called her at home—"How did you get my number?" It wasn't published in the phone book, and was available from the operator only if you knew her as Jenna Kendrick.

On impulse, Adam dialed directory assistance and was told the number was unlisted. The order had to have been processed sometime after last Wednesday. Why? Had his call made her feel vulnerable? Afraid?

The thought decided him. He couldn't take the chance that she didn't know about Barnes's parole. Somebody had to tell her. And since Roy Stevenson had flown to Cincinnati this afternoon before Adam could reach him, that somebody would have to be him.

Given a choice, he'd rather have strolled naked through a rattlesnake pit.

DINNER HAD GONE WELL, Jenna thought. At least she hadn't humiliated herself by dropping the pan of lasagna or dumping the salad in his lap or upchucking at the table. They hadn't talked much, but the silences weren't strained. She thought Adam seemed a little preoccupied—probably because he'd picked up on her nervousness and was trying to divine her mood.

She took the second bottle of wine and a couple of clean glasses with her when they moved into the living room. The two glasses she'd had with dinner had given her a pleasant buzz. One more glass, and she should be loose enough to launch into her confession.

She hadn't counted on the effects of *Casablanca*, which had just started when Adam turned on the television.

''One of the great movies of all time,'' he said as he sat beside her on the sofa. He poured himself some wine, leaned back, then abruptly swiveled to look into her eyes.

''Sorry, I should have asked. Did you have something else planned?''

Jenna sipped at her wine, taking a few seconds for self-assessment, and decided she wasn't quite ready to talk yet. "No," she murmured. "Nothing special."

His left eyebrow formed an inquisitive arch. "Sure? While we were eating, I had the feeling there was something on your mind."

"Mmm, well...as a matter of fact..." She reached for the wine and topped off her glass. This was going to be even harder than she'd thought. "But it can wait. *Casablanca* is one of my all-time favorites."

Which was true. And it had just occurred to her that watching it, with her, might put him in a romantic, forgiving frame of mind. Unfortunately, she failed to anticipate what her own response might be to watching the movie with him.

Adam casually eased his arm around her shoulders when Ilsa made her first entrance. By then Jenna was completely immersed in the story, and the contact felt so natural, so *right*, that she relaxed against his side.

By the time Rick returned to his apartment above the Café Américain to find Ilsa waiting, desperate for the letters of transit that would ensure Victor Lazlo's escape, Jenna's head was nestled in the crook of Adam's neck and both his arms were wrapped around her. She didn't know if it was the wine, or the film— such a heartbreaking mix of withheld secrets, misunderstanding and noble self-sacrifice—or her own frayed nerves, but when Ilsa finished spilling her guts and Rick took her in his arms, nothing short of an act of God could have stopped the tears that spilled from her eyes.

They didn't make it to the final scene. Adam turned to her in the middle of Bogart's "hill of beans" speech, sliding a hand under her hair to angle her head for his kiss. When his mouth closed softly on hers, Jenna instinctively reached out to draw him closer.

Her hands trembled as they caressed his head, his neck, the solid expanse of his shoulders. She was only vaguely aware of his quickened breathing and the fine tremors that betrayed the tenuous state of his self-control. A single thought tormented her: after tonight he might walk out of her life, leaving a horrible black emptiness that nothing and no one would ever fill.

For the past five years she had thought of herself as alone. But until now, this moment, she'd never fully comprehended the meaning of the word. This looming blackness was the worst thing she'd ever faced. She reacted with unconscious desperation, her touch increasingly urgent as she clung to Adam with a strength born of fear and frantic denial.

But suddenly he was wrenching away, burying his face in her hair. She felt his heart thundering against her breast, heard each harsh, labored breath as he struggled for control. It was a fight Jenna wanted him to lose. She twisted to nip at the clenched muscles along his jaw, and then higher, catching the lobe of his ear between her teeth, stroking it with the tip of her tongue. He jerked away again, but she felt the shudder that rippled through him.

"Stop."

It was more plea than command. Jenna dismissed it without an instant of doubt. Tonight might be all they had, all they would ever have, and she knew she wanted it. All of it, every last second.

"No." She breathed it into his ear, while her hands began to work on the buttons of his shirt. Adam reached to stop her, but his long, nimble fingers seemed to have lost their usual dexterity. Funny, she thought. Now he was the clumsy one, while her movements were deft and sure.

"Jenna, don't. This isn't—I shouldn't have—"

"Yes, it is," she contradicted.

Her voice sounded strange. It was amazingly steady, all things considered, but she was sure her vocal cords had never produced that low, husky throb before. She kept working on his buttons, pausing every few seconds to push his hands out of the way.

"And you should have," she murmured with an overt sensuality she hadn't known she was capable of. "I wanted you to."

She dispensed with the last button and slid her hands inside his shirt before he could stop her. He sucked in a sharp breath as her fingers splayed across his chest. She kissed his collarbone, rubbed her cheek against him, inhaling the aroma of soap and an intoxicating scent that she decided must be pure essence of Adam.

He didn't speak again, or try to restrain her, but neither did he give her any encouragement. That was all right. Jenna was cruising on instinct and intuition now, and her instincts were working just fine. She *knew* what he would like, what would give him pleasure. She'd been born knowing.

She trailed the nails of her left hand over his chest, raked them lightly across his washboard stomach; her right hand she dispatched to the snap of his jeans. It gave with a soft *pop*. Adam jerked as if he'd been shot at.

Jenna's lips curved against his chest in a feline smile of satisfaction. But a second later he grasped her head and pulled her up for a kiss that seared her soul and reduced her complacency to ashes. A ragged groan rose from somewhere deep inside him as his mouth hardened with need. It was a raw, primitive sound, uncivilized and uncivil. It should have alarmed her. Instead, it sent shivers of anticipation racing through her.

"I didn't mean for this to happen," he muttered between ravenous kisses.

"I know."

He finally let his hands roam where they would. "I must be crazy. I can't do this."

Jenna didn't bother to argue, not that he gave her the chance. She found the zipper of his jeans and eased the tab down, slowly and carefully, while Adam concentrated on freeing her from the blouse and slacks she'd spent the better part of an hour selecting. Her liberation was accomplished in scarcely more than a minute.

He took considerably more time removing her underwear. Too much time. Jenna wanted to tell him— no, *beg* him—to hurry, but she didn't have the breath. By the time her panties joined the other garments on the carpet, she was well past impatience and into fevered frenzy. She reached for him at the same time his arms locked around her and hauled her to him. They came together with the force of a head-on collision, mouths and bodies straining to overcome the fragile corporeal barriers that still separated them and fuse into a single being.

Suddenly Adam twisted, lifting her to sit astride his lap. The rough denim of his jeans rubbed against Jenna's thighs. She stopped breathing for an endless moment, and then he was inside her and instinct took over again.

"Remember this," he said in a hoarse whisper as he started to move. "When everything's gone to hell and you despise us both . . . remember."

Despise them both? The words scarcely registered. Was he quoting a line from the movie? It sounded like something Bogart's character would say. Her confusion only lasted an instant, though, before she was swept away on a surging tide that obliterated all thought.

Sometime later—minutes? hours?—she was aware of Adam lifting her, carrying her, gently lowering her onto the down-filled comforter on her bed. She stretched languorously and her fingers encountered the basset hound's soft plush body. She drew the dog to her breast with a dreamy smile.

"Oh, no," Adam muttered. Jenna opened her eyes in time to see him kick his jeans toward the door. "Two's company," he drawled, plucking the hound from her grasp and tossing it onto the dresser. His briefs followed the jeans. Jenna's smile evolved from dreamy to appreciative. When had he managed to dispense with his shirt, boots and socks?

"God, you're beautiful," she whispered as he joined her on the bed.

He flashed a devilish grin and kissed the end of her nose. "That's my line."

He stretched his leanly muscled body out beside her and reached for her. When he settled back with a contented sigh, she was lying half on top of him, his arms were around her, and her right leg was nestled between his legs. The arrangement suited Jenna fine. She slipped her arms around his waist and snuggled against his chest.

Neither of them spoke; words would have been superfluous. Far at the back of her mind, Jenna was aware that this blissful happiness couldn't last. Her fundamental dilemma hadn't changed or magically disappeared—eventually she was going to have to work up the courage to tell Adam the truth about herself. But not yet. She wanted to savor the peace and contentment, even if it was only illusory, for as long as possible.

They made love again, slowly this time, lingering over each wondrous new discovery, until the banked fires flared to life and urgency brought an end to their leisurely exploration. Afterwards, lying curled against Adam's side, Jenna was overwhelmed by anxiety and despair. The fear of losing him was ten times worse now... a hundred times worse. She should have told him everything, *before* they made love. What if he thought she'd thrown herself at him—and there was no denying she had—deliberately seduced him to gain some kind of emotional advantage?

Should she tell him now? Explain, before it was too late... if it wasn't already? No. These might be the last good memories she would have of their time together. She couldn't risk spoiling them. Tomorrow would be soon enough.

She fell asleep without intending to, and when her alarm went off she awoke to find Adam gone. On the dresser, a note was wedged under Adam, Jr.'s collar. It said simply: "Had to take care of some business. I'll call you."

COWARD.

The epithet had haunted Adam all day. He detested the word almost as much as the low-down feeling of disgrace, but there was no escaping either. The fact that Jenna had initiated their lovemaking didn't make him any less culpable in his own eyes. He should have taken control, of both the situation and his emotions.

He *should* have told her the truth, right away, or at least as soon as they'd finished dinner. He definitely *shouldn't* have turned on the television. Ten minutes into that damned movie, both his intentions and his willpower were distant memories. And it went without saying that he shouldn't have kissed her. But once he had...

The memory of Jenna's response was enough to resurrect his desire. It also strengthened his conviction that he'd been dead wrong about the kind of relationship she'd had with Dennis Barnes. Whoever Barnes had been sending messages to, it wasn't Jenna.

He consciously forced his thoughts from the emotional minefield his unprofessional conduct had created and focused on the job he'd been sent to do. A phone call to Washington yielded the information that Barnes had attended a dinner in his honor the previous night and had an appointment with his parole officer the following Tuesday, the day after Labor Day. That last news was especially heartening. Adam doubted that Barnes would risk taking any trips until after his initial appointment. A blatant parole violation so soon would guarantee him a one-way ticket back to prison.

The Justice Department still hadn't determined the identity of Barnes's female contact in St. Louis. Adam turned his attention in that direction. If Barnes did plan to come after Jenna, he would first take steps to decrease the risk factor. He'd have placed someone close to her—someone who could track her movements, become familiar with her normal routine.

A neighbor? Not likely. She wasn't especially friendly with any of them—didn't appear to have any close friends, in fact. Someone she worked with, then, saw every day. Possibly more than one someone.

In addition to Jenna, Adam had met three female employees at the Pendergrass agency. No doubt there were others. The sexpot—what was her name? Liza Roper. She'd struck him as a busybody, one of those chronically nosy women who's always up-to-date on the office gossip. A role that would serve her well if she'd been assigned to keep tabs on Jenna.

Then there was the middle-aged receptionist, Verda—though he was inclined to dismiss her as a prospect—and the other real estate agent, Ellie Something-or-other. They'd both been overtly curious when he showed up last Friday, but not so much so that they'd set off any alarms. Of course, anyone who was working undercover for Dennis Barnes would be good. She'd know how to blend into her surroundings, and she wouldn't do or say anything that might raise Jenna's suspicions.

Of the three, Liza Roper struck him as the most likely candidate. He would leave a message for Roy to run a background check on her. Meanwhile, he'd promised in the note he'd left that he would call Jenna. For the life of him, he didn't know what he would say to her.

DENNIS BARNES LOUNGED on a leather-upholstered wing chair in his host's luxurious living room. His prison uniform had been exchanged for fashionable pleated tan linen trousers and a French silk shirt. His wavy brown hair had been cut and styled, his nails manicured, the Rolex watch and gold signet ring restored. He appeared to be relaxed, completely at ease. His host, in contrast, was growing increasingly agitated as the minutes ticked by.

"I can't imagine why she isn't here," Nolan Matson remarked. "I specifically told her you expected her at two o'clock."

"Something must have come up," Barnes said coolly.

The pudgy banker didn't reply, but he was visibly distraught. He was accustomed to entertaining powerful people, wealthy people, even people who routinely conducted business on the wrong side of the law. But there were special dangers in welcoming this particular guest into his home. Not that there was any question about their physical safety. The large Tudor-style house sat in the middle of a two-acre tract that was enclosed by an eight-foot brick wall, and a private security firm constantly monitored a half-dozen video cameras that had been strategically placed around the grounds.

None of those safeguards allayed Matson's misgivings about holding the meeting at his private residence. It was entirely possible that Dennis Barnes had been followed, that at this very minute FBI or DEA agents were parked outside his front gate. Once they connected him to Barnes, it would be only a matter of time before they started digging and discovered that he'd been laundering money from questionable sources for years. They could and probably would confiscate everything—all his properties, the cars, the boat, even the jade and ivory carvings he'd spent a decade collecting.

He wished to God the woman would get here, so Barnes could conclude his business and leave. What was keeping her?

JENNA WAS COVERING Verda's desk while the receptionist had the stitches removed from her foot. Thankfully, she hadn't been called upon to do much more than take telephone messages; three of the agents were out showing properties and two others were attending a mortgage-insurance seminar. She was glad for the excuse to put off updating the monthly commission lists. She didn't think she'd be able to concentrate on calculating net profits and percentages this afternoon.

She'd been on pins and needles all day, waiting for Adam's call with a combination of anticipation and dread. When it finally came, she still wasn't prepared.

The first thing he said was, "Where's Verda?"

"At the doctor's." She blurted out the first thing that came to mind, mainly to delay the moment when he'd say whatever he'd called to say. "Did you get your business taken care of?"

There was a beat of dead silence, and she suddenly knew with agonizing, mortifying certainty that there hadn't been any business that needed taking care of. He'd slipped out of her bed in the middle of the night because he didn't want to be there when she woke up.

"Most of it." He paused again. Jenna squeezed her eyes shut and willed herself not to cry. "Last night..." he began. His voice was gruff, a little tentative, totally unlike his normal, laid-back drawl.

"I, uh..." Again he hesitated, cleared his throat. "Well, it was pretty damned incredible."

Jenna's eyes flew open. *Incredible?*

"Jenna? You still there?"

"Yes." A bud of warmth slowly unfolded in her chest. "Yes, it was," she murmured.

He exhaled a harsh breath. "I'm sorry I took off like that. To be honest, what happened... It really knocked me for a loop. I'm afraid I wasn't thinking straight."

Jenna's mouth curved in a rueful smile. "I can relate to that."

"There are things I have to tell you..." He trailed off. She had the feeling he was searching for the right words. Then he added in a surprisingly flat, unemotional tone, "We need to talk."

"I agree," she said quietly. There were things *he* had to tell *her?* Wait'll he heard what she had to tell him.

"Tonight." He didn't sound as if he was looking forward to the conversation. "I have to meet with some people this afternoon. It may take a while. How about if I pick up a pizza and come by about seven?"

Jenna said seven would be fine. After she hung up, she automatically glanced at her watch. A little more than four more hours, and then this awful tension and uncertainty would be over. One way or another.

DENNIS BARNES LEANED over the highly polished rosewood dining table, his weight on his outstretched arms as he studied the assortment of color photos.

"She's gained a little weight," he observed dispassionately.

"And her hair's longer," Verda Young pointed out.

She stood at Barnes's right, occasionally directing his attention to one of the photos she'd brought. In addition to a half-dozen candid shots of Jenna, the collection included several eight-by-ten enlargements of her car and house, taken from various angles and at different times of the day and night.

"Notice that several of the neighbors park their cars on the street. So long as you don't hang around too long, you shouldn't attract attention."

Nolan Matson abruptly ended his uneasy silence. "I still think it's unnecessarily dangerous for you to go yourself, Dennis. Why not send Frank instead?"

Verda audibly sucked in her breath.

"Out of the question," Barnes replied coolly. "Not only is he unreliable, he's also a coward."

"But this woman is under the protection of the Marshals Service, and they know about your parole," Matson pointed out. "What if they've assigned someone to keep an eye on her?"

"They haven't," Verda said flatly. "They check up on her every few weeks, but they're careful not to make public contact. The whole point of the Witness

Security Program is to protect the new identities of the people enrolled in it."

The banker waved a hand in impatience. "I know you've spent the last three years studying every aspect of the woman's life, Verda, but you haven't been able to keep tabs on her twenty-four hours a day. What if she's made friends with some new neighbors and decides to invite them over for dinner, or—"

She cut him off, her voice terse. "I've already covered this ground, Nolan. She goes out of her way *not* to make friends. She keeps everybody at a distance, even the people she works with five days a week, and *especially* people she's just met. She doesn't trust anybody."

"What about this writer?" he persisted. "You say he just breezed in one day to buy an insurance policy and suddenly she's seeing him virtually every night. We know nothing about the man. He could be a plant—FBI or DEA."

"He's not a plant!" Verda snapped.

"You can't *know* that! I tell you, it's foolishly reckless to think Dennis can just stroll up to her front door—"

"That's enough."

Barnes's quiet baritone halted their bickering as effectively as if he'd dropped a live grenade between them. His hard, cold gaze swung from Verda to Matson, who unconsciously backed up a step.

"I trust Verda's judgment," Barnes said levelly. "She knows what the consequences would be for providing me with faulty or inadequate information." He paused a moment, allowing them both to absorb the implied threat, then continued in the same chillingly soft tone.

"You don't seem to understand, Nolan. This isn't business, it's personal. Not only did this woman betray me, she's also responsible for the deaths of my wife and son. This is one debt no one else can collect for me."

Chapter Six

After work, Jenna decided to run some errands, to keep mind and body occupied until Adam arrived. She collected a bundle of clothes to drop off at the cleaners, then spent half an hour taking inventory of the refrigerator and cupboards and making a shopping list. It was a few minutes past six, still full daylight, when she backed her Escort out of the driveway.

ADAM SAT LEANING forward, his expression taut as he listened to the hollow voice coming from Roy Stevenson's speaker phone. Roy was slouched in his swivel chair behind the desk, fingers steepled in front of his mouth. He displayed no reaction to the news they'd just received, but Adam knew he was steamed. He didn't even try to blunt the anger in his own voice.

"So you're telling us Barnes has disappeared." Roy lowered his hands and shook his head, his forehead creased in a frown.

Adam ignored the silent warning. "I thought you guys had him under twenty-four-hour surveillance."

The FBI agent on the other end of the line responded testily. "We did, and he knew it. We're confident he hasn't strayed far from home. It would be a clear violation of the terms of his parole. We suspect he's playing a little hide-and-seek, thumbing his nose at us. He'll turn up in a day or two.''

"Probably with a dozen witnesses in tow who'll swear he never left his estate," Roy put in dryly.

"I wouldn't be a bit surprised," the agent muttered. "In any case, we'll keep you informed."

"See that you do," Roy replied, and terminated the connection. "Hide-and-seek, my ass," he said scornfully. "Damned Fibbers. I wouldn't trust 'em to keep an eye on Mount Rushmore."

"He could be on the way here," Adam murmured, more to himself than to Roy. "He may be here already."

"We'd better get our act together, just in case," Roy said with his usual equanimity. He lifted the receiver and punched an intercom button. "Marv, I need to see you."

Less than a minute later a tall, genial-looking young man with sandy hair strolled into the office. He nodded an impersonal greeting to Adam, then turned to Roy.

"What's up?"

Roy gestured toward the vacant armchair beside Adam, and when the young man was seated introduced him as Marvin Bolander, a rookie marshal who'd been assigned to the St. Louis office a few weeks earlier.

"Adam's with the Criminal Division," Roy explained.

Marv smiled as he leaned forward to shake hands. "OCR Section, right? You're one of the guys who're trying to arrange long-term federal housing for Dennis Barnes. Good to meet you.''

"Marv installed that alarm you noticed at Jenna's house,'' Roy said. "We've had an intercept on her phone line for the past week, since it became clear that Barnes would get his parole. When she called a private security firm, I made the decision to intervene.''

Adam's brows jerked together in a scowl. Roy held up a hand. "Spare me the lecture about her civil rights,'' he said crisply. "My number-one priority was and is protecting her life. Anyway, the owner of the firm was happy to cooperate. He still gets paid, and we were able to get an alarm installed the next day. She'd have had to wait at least a week for him to fit her in.''

"I gave her your basic eardrum-perforating siren,'' Marv put in. "We figured anything fancy—heat and motion detectors, infrared cameras—would be over-kill. Besides, she couldn't afford any of that stuff.''

"And since she hadn't come to us in the first place, we were afraid we'd make her suspicious if we offered a lot of high-tech equipment for a bargain-basement price,'' Roy added. "Marv's scheduled to go back to-morrow and replace the alarm she's got with something a little more sophisticated.''

"And none too soon,'' Adam muttered. When Roy had finished briefing Marvin on Dennis Barnes's disappearance, he asked, "Why *didn't* she come to you?''

Roy sat back in his chair and released a frustrated sigh. "Obviously, she doesn't think she can trust us to protect her.''

Yes, Adam thought. Obviously. He was glad Roy had stepped in and made sure Jenna had at least a basic alarm system, but was troubled by her lack of confidence in the Marshals Service. Did she distrust all law-enforcement types, he wondered bleakly, or only those who worked for the Justice Department?

BARNES SCOUTED the block twice, spacing his circuits fifteen minutes apart, before he parked the borrowed car in front of a house across the street and four doors up from Jenna's. The single-story brick ranch was empty, the twin porch lights and a table lamp in the living room connected to timers which turned them on at dusk. The owners wouldn't be coming out to check on the strange car. They were on a Caribbean cruise. Verda's information had been detailed and, so far, one-hundred-percent accurate. He had expected no less.

Jenna had returned home just as he swung past on the second circuit. He'd gone around once more to give her time to get inside. His luck was holding. The street was empty—no one walking the family dog, no kids riding skateboards or roller skating. The aroma of meat being seared on a backyard grill drifted through the car's open windows.

He checked his Rolex. Just past seven. Not quite dark enough, but maybe he should make his move now, instead of waiting. He didn't like sitting out in the open, on display for anybody who happened by.

He became aware that his palms were sweating. Anticipation was a sharp, metallic taste in his mouth and impatience lay coiled inside him like a spring wound too tight, jeopardizing his clarity and focus. He closed his eyes, concentrating on taking slow, deep breaths. He'd waited five years for this. He couldn't allow his lust for revenge to ruin everything now.

He waited a minute more to be sure he had complete control, then opened the door and stepped out of the car.

ADAM HAD CALLED FROM the pizzeria shortly before seven to say he'd be a little late and to ask if she wanted mushrooms or hot peppers. Jenna vetoed both, certain her stomach would refuse to tolerate either. She finished putting away the groceries and set out plates, forks and paper napkins, then went to the living room to turn on the porch light.

She was peering through the fanlight in the front door as she switched on the light, hoping for a glimpse of Adam's Mustang. Preoccupied, her attention on the street, she probably wouldn't have noticed the darker silhouette gliding through the lengthening shadows to the right of the porch, if it hadn't abruptly stopped moving when the light came on. Even after she picked up the shape from the corner of her eye, she almost identified it as the shadow of a tree limb or shrub swaying in the wind.

Except...

She stopped breathing, her gaze shifting to the dark figure suspended in the gloom beyond the porch light's reach.

There wasn't any wind.

The figure moved at the same instant the thought flashed across her mind. In the two or three seconds before it reached the cone of light, something else occurred to her, a realization that left her stunned and dizzy with fear. Yesterday had been the date of Dennis Barnes's parole hearing.

How could she have forgotten! How could she have let the date sneak up on her like that?

The amorphous shadow moved onto the porch, resolving itself first into human form and then, as horror swept through Jenna, taking the shape of a man.

A man she knew.

A nightmare come to life.

Her breath shuddered free on a sob of pure terror. He was here. *Here!* After years of watching and waiting, knowing this day would come and that if she wasn't ready she would die, she'd let him catch her alone and unprepared.

Her hand scrabbled across the door, instinctively checking the dead-bolt lock. Barnes stopped in the center of the porch, no more than four feet away, allowing the light to fully illuminate his face. He looked straight into the fanlight.

Jenna shoved away from the door with a strangled gasp. *The phone! Call the police!* She sprinted to the kitchen, yanked the handset off the hook.

Nothing. No dial tone, not even white noise.

"Kendra."

At first she thought her mind had fabricated the voice from the fear pumping through her. But then it came again, soft and relentless, addressing her by the name she hadn't used in five years.

"Come now, Kendra. Surely you're not surprised to see me."

She dropped the phone and clapped her hands over her ears, her gaze flying around the kitchen for something she could use as a weapon. A knife, a screwdriver...anything.

"You knew I'd come."

The living room window! She could hear him so clearly because she'd opened it a couple of inches when she came home from work, to air out the house. If he noticed—Jenna lunged for the drawer next to the stove, tugged it open, rummaged among the utensils and serving pieces.

"I might have forgiven you for the five years you stole from me, Kendra. But never for Kayla and Thad. They're dead because of you."

The indictment sliced into a vein of deeply buried guilt and summoned the specters of her sister and nephew. She slumped over the drawer with a piteous moan.

"They *burned,* Kendra."

Oh, God. Don't listen! *Don't listen!* She pushed herself upright. Her scrabbling fingers closed on the handle of a long-tined meat fork.

"Before I'm finished—" his cultured voice coarsened with hate "—you're going to wish you'd burned with them."

Clutching the fork in her right hand, Jenna hit the switch for the kitchen light and eased through the arched doorway to the living room. The floor lamp next to her reading chair was on, but it was between her and the door. Hoping he couldn't see past the glare, she kept her back pressed against the wall and inched forward. Could he see her? Hear her harsh, shallow breathing?

Think! she ordered herself to ward off the panic that threatened to paralyze her. *What are your options?*

The bedroom, bath and a small utility room were behind her, at the rear of the house. She briefly considered slipping back into the kitchen and from there out the side door in the utility room, but abandoned the idea when she remembered that the hinges screeched like banshees when the door was opened. She'd been meaning to oil them for weeks. She could duck into the bedroom and try to get out one of the windows, but that would mean turning her back on Barnes, boxing herself into a corner. And what if he'd brought one of his goons with him to watch the back of the house?

She closed her eyes in abject despair. So much for her options. This was it, then. In another minute he would break down the door, or rip the screen off the opened window, and she would have to try to fight him off with a barbecue fork. A hysterical sob tore at her throat and she started to shake uncontrollably.

The next second an ear-splitting noise erupted at the front of the house. Jenna jerked so violently in reaction that her head and shoulders banged into the wall. Almost immediately a voice penetrated the appalling din—a man's voice, raised in fury, swearing savagely—and then there were three booming thuds.

Jenna stayed where she was, her back flattened against the wall, while her heart gradually slowed its frantic pounding. The burglar alarm! She'd completely forgotten about it. She must have automatically set it when she'd carried in the groceries.

When it dawned on her that the cursing and banging had stopped, she stepped away from the wall, hesitantly at first, her legs as unsteady as a toddler's. The thuds had unmistakably been Barnes's enraged fist striking the door. But was he still there, or had the alarm driven him away?

She crept forward, careful to stay to the right of the fanlight. The alarm continued its high-pitched scream, making it impossible to pick up any other sounds. She was about three feet from the door when she noticed the doorknob rattling as if someone was trying to wrench the entire lockset out of the wood. She flinched and shrank back.

"Go away!" she shouted. "I have a gun. So help me God, I'll shoot through the door."

The knob stopped moving at once. Jenna released a shaky breath. "I mean it!" She channeled every ounce of strength she possessed into her voice. "If you touch the door again, I'll shoot!"

"Jenna, it's me," a familiar voice called. "Don't shoot, okay? He's gone."

Adam!

Her knees almost buckled. She dropped the fork, stumbled to the door and leaned against it while she released the dead bolt. He pushed inside so fast he almost knocked her down, but somehow he got his arms around her while she was tottering, and hauled her to his chest. She collapsed against him, letting him take her weight.

"Are you all right?"

His voice was a hoarse rasp in her ear. She nodded mutely. She was shaking too hard to speak.

"How do you turn off that damned alarm?"

Physically Jenna felt drained, as weak as a newborn kitten, but her mind was already leaping ahead, forecasting consequences. Had Adam seen Barnes? More important, had Barnes seen Adam? She stilled the quaking of her body by sheer force of will, straightened and stepped away from him to turn off the alarm. Through the open door, she saw that three of her neighbors had come out of their houses and were standing on the sidewalk and her lawn.

"You all right, Miz Kendrick?" old Mr. Parsons from next door asked in concern.

"Yes. Thank you," she answered, forcing a weak smile. "Just shaken up."

"I'd dozed off in front of the TV, and that air-raid siren woke me up," he explained. "It sure did the job. That fella that was tryin' t'break in took off like a scalded cat. Saw him tear across your driveway from my front window."

"He ran up the block and jumped in a car parked in front of the Greenbergs'," Mrs. Thompson from across the street put in.

A teenaged boy who lived three doors up stood behind her, his eyes as big as silver dollars. "It happened so fast I didn't get a good look at him or the car, but I called the police, anyway."

"So'd I," Mr. Parsons said. "Guess now we'll see how fast they come when they're called." He gave Adam a suspicious once-over. "You sure you're okay?"

Jenna nodded. "I'm fine, really. The only damage done was to my nerves."

She was suddenly overwhelmed by a strange combination of gratitude and anxiety that brought her close to tears. She'd never said more than a dozen words to any of these people, yet they'd come out of their homes after dark, apparently prepared to confront a possibly dangerous prowler and give her whatever comfort or assistance they could. She was humbled and touched by their concern. At the same time, the knowledge that two of them had already called the police filled her with apprehension. The police would no doubt ask if she'd recognized the burglar, whether he was someone she knew, someone who might have a grudge against her. Could she lie convincingly?

As if he sensed her distress, Adam slipped a supportive arm around her waist as he murmured, "Looks like the cops have a pretty good response time in this part of town."

A patrol car, siren silent but light bar flashing, had just turned the corner at the end of the block.

"Well, now, that ain't half bad," Mr. Parsons said in approval as the car braked to a halt at the curb in front of Jenna's house.

AN HOUR AND A HALF LATER, Jenna was thinking it had been easier and certainly less stressful dealing with the two officers who responded to her neighbors' calls than with Adam.

Maybe it was some kind of possessive macho thing, but he was reacting much more forcefully than she'd expected. He still radiated angry tension, his rugged features set in a grimly forbidding expression and his hands unconsciously flexing into fists as he prowled the house. While Jenna couldn't deny that a part of her was gratified by his fussing and fretting, his agitation was feeding her own, at a time when she needed to be calm and centered, to think and plan.

"The lock on that side door wouldn't stop a determined eight-year-old," he said as he stalked back into the kitchen.

Jenna laid the slice of pizza she'd been about to bite into back on her plate. "I know. Why don't you sit down and have some pizza."

"And the locks on your windows are a joke."

"Adam, please—"

"I want you to pack an overnight bag. You can stay with me tonight."

She stared at him blankly for a moment, then lowered her gaze to her fingers, which she slowly wiped on a paper napkin. She'd already decided to leave the house, but staying with Adam was out of the question. He'd told the policemen that he had just pulled up when Dennis Barnes came running across her lawn and into the street. He'd got a good look at Barnes— good enough to provide an amazingly accurate physical description—which meant Barnes had been close enough to get a good look at him.

At this moment Barnes might be assigning someone to check Adam out. One of his hired hands could be watching her house, waiting to follow him home. It was even possible that one of her neighbors was on Barnes's payroll. That could explain his incredible timing; he'd managed to arrive minutes after she returned home.

No, she couldn't stay with Adam. The simple fact that he'd shown up when he did had probably earned him a place on Barnes's list of enemies. She couldn't— wouldn't—put him in even more danger. She had to start distancing herself from him now, agonizing as that would be.

Which meant that telling him about her past, about Barnes, was also out of the question. Because, judging by his proprietary, take-charge attitude since the police left, she suspected he would insist on staying at her side twenty-four hours a day if he knew. She became aware that he was watching her intently, waiting for her response.

"Don't you think you're overreacting just a bit?" she asked, lifting the pizza slice and taking a big bite.

His eyes narrowed incredulously. "No. I damn well don't. The son of a bitch might come back."

Jenna's mouth went dry. There was no *might* about it. The son of a bitch *would* come back, sooner or later. Determined that Adam wouldn't know how the thought terrified her, she took a sip of wine to wash down the pizza.

Apparently angered by her silence, he snatched up the meat fork he'd collected from the living room floor. "Of course, you could always threaten him with your 'gun.'"

His sarcastic, mocking tone grated on her already raw nerves. "It worked with you, didn't it?" she retorted.

Then, because she knew he was only thinking of her safety and she didn't want to argue with him, especially tonight, she drew a deep breath and gave him a conciliatory smile.

"I guess it would probably be a good idea to stay somewhere else, at least until I can get new locks installed. But if I remember correctly, Tex, you described your place as not much bigger than a cigar box."

"All right, then, I'll take you to a motel," he said without missing a beat.

Which, of course, was what Jenna had been leading up to. She pretended to consider the suggestion for a few seconds before acceding with a nod. "Okay. But only for a night or two."

ADAM WAS JUST ABOUT at the end of his rope. For a while there, he'd thought he would have to blast her out of the damned house with dynamite.

He didn't trust her composure. It was an act, he knew it in his gut. She'd been so terrified when he first arrived that he'd half expected her to start packing before the police finished taking statements. Instead, she'd suddenly acquired an unnatural, almost stoic calm. When the cops left, she expressed her appreciation to her neighbors, then matter-of-factly collected the pizza from his car and brought it in to warm it in the microwave.

But Adam wasn't buying her cool, everything's-fine-now-let's-put-this-unpleasantness-behind-us act, for one very good reason: If she hadn't trusted the Marshals Service to protect her before Barnes showed up at her front door, she sure as hell wasn't going to trust them now. She was up to something. Adam knew it as surely as he knew Dennis Barnes was still a free man because he had screwed up.

It had happened in the split second when he recognized Barnes and had to decide whether to go after him or make sure Jenna was all right. There was no doubt in his mind that he could have caught Barnes, but the need to assure himself that Jenna hadn't been hurt was more compelling. If he'd responded rationally instead of emotionally, Barnes would be a guest of St. Louis County now, maybe even already in federal custody and en route back to Maryland, and he and Jenna could be sorting out their differences.

Differences. Now there was an understatement, he thought bitterly. The barriers between them made China's Great Wall look like a speed bump.

What bothered him most was that they weren't talking. At least, not about anything that mattered. Neither of them had said a word about last night. It was as if they'd both decided to pretend it hadn't happened. Adam hadn't decided any such thing, but for the life of him he couldn't think of a way to broach the subject.

"I realize you're upset about that maniac trying to break into your house and murder you, but I just wanted to say, for the record, that making love with you was the most fantastic, mind-blowing experience of my life" hardly seemed appropriate. Or adequate.

But troubling as their failure to even acknowledge last night's intimacy was, it was Jenna's deliberate, calculated withdrawal that set off his intuitive alarms. Obviously it wasn't only the Marshals Service she didn't trust. He'd felt her growing more distant as the night wore on. Why? The question plagued him. He didn't dare confront her, afraid he'd push her even farther away, but he sensed that her reserve was more than just a reaction to the trauma of unexpectedly coming face-to-face with Barnes.

She wasn't not talking because she was in shock, or because she simply had nothing to say. There was a secretive quality to her silence. She was considering, deliberating.

Planning.

The insight hit him like a bolt out of the blue. That was it—she was working on some kind of plan. And whatever it was, she had no intention of taking him into her confidence.

As soon as she was installed for the night in a motel near Forest Park, he went to the pay phone in the lobby and called Roy Stevenson at home. Then he moved his car to a parking spot from which he could keep an eye on the door to Jenna's room. Marvin Bolander arrived to relieve him twenty minutes later.

JENNA CHECKED OUT of the motel at six-fifteen the next morning and had the desk clerk call a cab to take her home. She'd set the alarm for five-thirty, knowing she would have to make an early start in order to accomplish everything she needed to get done today.

She'd been right not to place her unconditional trust in the Marshals Service. They'd done their best, but their best hadn't been good enough. She'd always doubted that it would be, so she'd devised her own plan, a plan that would be ready to set in motion when Dennis Barnes came after her.

She carried the overnight bag into her bedroom and unpacked, then pulled a large plastic box from under the bed. Jenna lifted out several neatly folded sweaters to get at the small, fireproof document safe at the bottom of the box. She quickly spun through the numbers of the combination lock, lifted the lid and removed a manila envelope, the only item the safe contained. Then she closed the safe and carefully arranged the sweaters on top of it before shoving the box back under the bed.

She emptied her shoulder bag onto the bed and put the manila envelope at the bottom. Tears welled in her eyes as she tossed the odds and ends back into the bag, but she angrily wiped them away. She couldn't afford sentiment now. Her survival depended on staying cool, alert and, above all, unemotional. She mustn't think about what she was leaving behind. She especially mustn't think about Adam.

She resisted the urge to wander through the house one last time. There was something in every room that she would be tempted to take with her, something that might be missed later, when the marshals collected everything for storage or auction. But at the last minute, as she was about to leave the bedroom, she saw the stuffed basset hound. He was still on the dresser, where Adam had tossed him the night before last.

For a moment she hesitated. She'd promised herself she wouldn't take *anything* from the house. But except for her memories, Adam, Jr., was all she would ever have of Adam. And who would know? She picked up the dog and stuffed it into her bag, then walked out of the small rented house that had been home for the last five years.

Chapter Seven

She shouldn't have taken Adam, Jr. Just having him in the car stirred up painful memories and unleashed a storm of unwanted emotions.

The dog's soft brown muzzle poked out of her shoulder bag, his soulful eyes both imploring and accusing as he observed her from the passenger seat. How could she walk away from Adam without so much as a word of explanation? he seemed to say. She'd never even told him how she felt, never said the words *I love you.*

The stuffed dog made a mean devil's advocate. It was true, Adam didn't deserve what she was going to do to him, and God knew she didn't want to do it. They deserved a chance, at least, to find out if they could overcome her past and build a life together.

"All right, you win," she said to the hound as she steered into the exit lane. "I'll give Uncle Roy one last chance before I bail out."

When she arrived at work she opened the building, reset the thermostat, started a pot of coffee...following her usual routine, as if it was just another workday.

By nine, all the staff except Verda and Frank Pendergrass had arrived and were busy munching donuts, sipping coffee and grumbling about having to
work on such a glorious day. The consensus was that
the Labor Day weekend should include Friday as well
as the following Monday. Jenna kept busy at her desk,
listening to the background chatter without joining in.
She'd forgotten that it was a long holiday weekend.
That should work to her advantage, if Roy Stevenson
failed to come through for her.

Frank waddled in at a quarter past nine, muttering
a brusque "Morning" as he passed Jenna's desk. Must
have been a late poker game, she thought derisively.
Working for Frank was one part of this life she
wouldn't miss. When Verda Young still hadn't shown
up by nine-thirty, Jenna began to worry. She'd
planned to leave the agency before ten and had
counted on asking the receptionist to fill in for her
until after lunch. She found Verda's home number in
the Rolodex and was about to call to check on her,
when the phone rang. It was Verda.

"Jenna?" The older woman's speech was slurred
and thick, as if she had a mouthful of marbles. "I
won't be in today. I had a little fender bender last night
and I'm so stiff and sore I can hardly move. Not to
mention I've got a black eye and my jaw's swollen up
like a grapefruit. Anyway, I know Frank wouldn't
want me sitting at the front desk looking like this. I'd
scare people away."

Jenna assured Verda that they would manage until
she felt well enough to come back to work, then went
to tell Frank that his receptionist would be taking a
few days off.

"Had a wreck, huh?" He shuffled papers on his desk, displaying neither dismay nor concern, not even bothering to look up when he received the news. "Well, I guess you'll have to fill in for her till she comes back."

"You're all heart, Frank," Jenna said. The comment provoked an irritable grunt, but he still didn't lift his eyes from the papers—probably threatening letters from people he owed money to. "I have to leave in a few minutes for a dentist's appointment. I'll ask Liza to cover Verda's desk while I'm out."

"Fine," Frank muttered with a nod. "You do that."

Jenna gave him a disgusted look, which unfortunately he didn't see, before she left his office. She'd have liked to tell him exactly what she thought of him, as well, but she resisted the urge. Everything about today had to appear normal; she mustn't do anything out of the ordinary, and that included flinging insults at her boss.

She left her car in a parking lot just off Market Street, a couple of blocks from the Marshals Service office. There was no sign of Roy's secretary. Jenna took a seat in the outer office and hoped she wouldn't have to wait long—and that this impulsive side trip wouldn't turn out to be a waste of time.

She intended to tell Roy that Dennis Barnes had come after her and demand that he either give her round-the-clock protection or relocate her until Barnes was caught. She also intended to tell him about Adam. She didn't relish the idea of confiding in him about her personal life; she had precious little privacy, as it was. But if Roy convinced her that he and his staff could protect her from Barnes, she would ask him to speak to Adam, to explain the Witness Security Program and how she had come to be enrolled in it. She had no idea how Adam was going to react when he learned about her past, but she figured having a United States Marshal serve as her advocate couldn't hurt.

A raised male voice alerted her that the door to Roy's office was slightly ajar. Jenna tried not to listen. She had enough troubles of her own. She certainly didn't want to become an unintentional eavesdropper to someone else's, and heaven knew what kind of criminal activity was being discussed.

Unfortunately, as the man became more agitated, his voice rose to a level that was impossible to block out. Apparently he was also pacing, because his angry harangue sounded intermittently closer and then farther away, then closer again.

Jenna closed her eyes and tried to think of something to distract herself. But then she caught the end of a sentence that broke her concentration and brought a reluctant smile to her lips.

"—dammit, those morons couldn't find their collective asses with both hands and an anatomy chart!"

Now who did that sardonic drawl remind her of? she thought wryly. A second later Roy Stevenson's even-tempered reply cut her amusement short and caused her to snap upright in the chair.

"Calm down, Adam. They're doing everything that can be done."

The first man responded with a single succinct cussword. Jenna leaned forward, unconsciously clenching both hands on the strap of her shoulder bag. Was that *her* Adam?

"He can't leave St. Louis without being spotted," Roy insisted.

"He doesn't intend to leave St. Louis, Roy. He intends to kill Jenna."

Jenna's breath caught painfully. She'd never heard that emotion in his voice—sarcasm so corrosive it could have etched glass—but the reference to her eliminated any doubt that it was Adam.

"She's here," he continued grimly. "In St. Louis. Believe me, Barnes isn't going anywhere so long as there's a chance he can get at her."

"His parole—"

"He isn't thinking about his parole, dammit! The man's a psychopathic megalomaniac, and he's obsessed with revenge. It's the only thing he cares about, all he dreams about when he goes to sleep. We have to throw everything we've got into finding him, *now*, before he goes after her again."

Jenna listened in stunned, frozen silence. He'd known about Barnes's parole, known Barnes would come after her. He'd *known!* Everything. All along. He'd deliberately deceived her.... *Please, God, let this be a bad dream.* But then came that damning "We have to throw everything we've got into finding him...."

We! She suddenly felt dizzy and sick to her stomach.

"What about his local contacts?" he was asking Roy.

"The FBI's covering that."

"Screw the FBI! I can get the list from Washington. We can start—"

"No, Adam," Roy interrupted firmly. "I warned you in the beginning not to turn this into a personal crusade. I know you think the government threw away the case you'd built five years ago, but it was a judgment call. Prosecutors have to make them all the time. Give it up. It's ancient history. At least we got a conviction on the racketeering charges, thanks to Jenna's testimony. And while I'm on the subject, you're dead wrong about her, always have been. She didn't conspire with Barnes to secure the lesser charges."

There was more, but Jenna didn't stay to hear it. She had to get out of the office, the building, before she completely fell apart. She met Roy's secretary in the hall and almost knocked the woman down in her hurry to reach the elevator. Later she would realize that it was a miracle she hadn't been run over crossing the street, or driven head-on into a bus. She must have been on autopilot, reflexes taking over while her brain labored to process the things she'd heard in Roy Stevenson's office.

Adam was one of them, some kind of agent for the Justice Department.

He'd known everything—about her, about Barnes—all along. Before he'd strolled into the agency and asked for "renter's insurance," before she'd noticed him in the tavern, before he'd even come to St. Louis. Before *she'd* come to St. Louis.

He'd deliberately lied to her, set out to use her! Made her fall in love with him.

She wanted to rage at him, pound him with her fists—No, something that would do more damage, something that would inflict on him the same pain she was feeling.

She wanted to die.

She gradually became aware that her face was wet, and that she was sitting in her car in a parking garage near the river. She pried her fingers from the steering wheel. The ticket stub she'd been issued at the garage's street-level entrance lay crumpled and damp on her left palm. She shoved it into her bag and dug out a packet of tissues, dried her face, blew her nose. The basset hound watched with sad, sympathetic eyes.

"Damn him!" she said to the toy. "Damn him to hell!"

Something inside her died as she said the words, like a flame that had been snuffed out. When she left the car, she was calm and composed. Her eyes were dry, her mind was clear, and her heart was a black, frozen lump in her chest.

WHEN ADAM RETURNED to Roy Stevenson's office, Roy was still slicing Marvin Bolander into small pieces, and the rookie marshal was still stoically accepting the reprimand. Roy halted his tirade to snap out anxiously, "Did you catch her?"

Adam shook his head. "She'd disappeared by the time I got downstairs."

"Why don't I go check her house?" Marv suggested.

"Good idea," Adam said before Roy could tear into the young man again.

Marv bobbed his head and pivoted toward the door, but Roy stopped him with a curt "Hold it! Who's in charge of this office?"

"You are," Adam said quietly. "He knows he fumbled the ball. Give him a chance to redeem himself."

"All right," Roy muttered after a moment. "But if you find her, you'd damned well better not lose her again."

"You think I was too rough on him," he said when the younger man had gone.

Adam grimaced. "I think there's plenty of blame to go around."

When Roy's secretary had returned to the office with a stack of reports and faxes, she'd mentioned running into an obviously distraught Jenna Kendrick in the hall. As soon as she described the woman, Adam and Roy had realized that Jenna must have heard them talking about Barnes, and about her. But when Adam was about to go after her, Roy dissuaded him with the admonition that she probably wouldn't welcome him with open arms until she'd had some time to cool down and the reminder that Marvin was keeping her under surveillance.

But then Marvin phoned a couple of minutes later to ask if Jenna was still in Roy's office. Having followed her that far, he'd decided it would be safe to take a break—his first in more than twelve hours. He was ordering coffee and a Danish to go in the coffee shop on the ground floor when she'd left the building. If he'd been looking toward the large windows at the front of the shop, he'd have seen her.

Yes, Adam thought grimly, there was plenty of blame to go around. But most of it was his.

How much had she heard? Enough to make her run, obviously. From him? The question had been gnawing at him ever since Roy's secretary dropped her little bombshell.

Roy's voice broke into his tormented thoughts. "Somebody should check the office where she works, in case she went back there."

Adam shook off the anxiety that had settled over him like a heavy, suffocating cloak. "Yeah, right. I'll go."

"You sure?" Roy was looking at him in concern. No wonder, after the things that had spilled out of him less than ten minutes ago—apparently just *after* Jenna ran out of the office. "I can send somebody else or go myself."

"No. Nobody will think anything of it if I show up in the middle of the day." His voice deepened, hardened. "Besides, I want to talk to Verda Young."

"Don't tip your hand," Roy warned as he left the office. Adam didn't bother to reply.

The background check on Liza Roper had turned up zilch. She'd never had so much as a parking ticket, and nothing in her history suggested she'd ever come in contact with Barnes or any of his associates.

But a superficial investigation of Verda Young had been more rewarding. Verda, it turned out, had served two years of a five-year sentence for tax fraud. The company she'd worked for at the time of her conviction just happened to be owned by none other than Dennis Barnes. Adam had cursed himself when he scanned the one-page report. He should have known; the woman's very drabness should have tipped him off. Of course Barnes wouldn't have chosen someone as conspicuous as Liza Roper.

If Jenna had returned to the agency, he would warn her about Verda. Assuming, of course, that she was in the mood to listen to anything he had to say. And then he wanted five minutes with the Pendergrasses' receptionist. Not to interrogate her—Roy didn't have to worry that he'd do something stupid, alert her that they were on to her. But maybe he could trick her into giving some indication where Barnes was holed up. Unfortunately, neither of the women he'd hoped to find at the agency was there.

"Jen had a dentist's appointment, and Verda wrecked her car last night," Liza Roper told him between answering the phone and scribbling terse, illegible messages. "She called in this morning, said she was black-and-blue and too sore to get out of bed."

Barnes, Adam thought. He'd probably punished Verda for not knowing about the recently installed alarm on Jenna's front door.

"Did Jenna say how long she expected her appointment to take?" he asked, hoping against hope that she really had gone to the dentist's.

"Uh-uh," Liza said. "But she left a little before ten, so she should've been back by now." Then, her beautiful eyes widening in concern, she added, "I hope he didn't break her jaw or something. That happened to a friend of mine once. She was off work for two weeks."

When Adam returned to Roy's office, he got the name of Jenna's dentist from her file and called the man's office. As he'd half expected, she had no appointment scheduled that day. He'd just got off the phone when Marv called in to report that she hadn't returned to her house. Roy ordered him to stay put, just in case she showed up.

Adam stood at one of the tall windows in Roy's office, staring down at the traffic on Market Street. He'd passed beyond worry, into stomach-churning fear. Jenna was out there. Somewhere. And so was Dennis Barnes.

THE NORTH-SIDE MOTEL just off I-70 was shabby, but clean. Not that it mattered. Jenna paid for only one night and stayed just long enough to use the bathroom. Stashing the room key in her purse, she walked to a nearby bus stop, rode back downtown and hailed a cab to take her to a car-rental agency. She drove off the lot in a two-year-old Plymouth.

Twenty minutes later she checked into another motel, off I-40 in Richmond Heights. She gave the young woman at the registration desk the same credit card she'd presented at the north-side motel and the car-rental agency. The name on the card was Susan Devers. The same name was on most of the identification she'd removed from the manila envelope—the envelope which had resided in a document safe under her bed for almost five years and was now in a litter barrel in a downtown parking garage.

This motel obviously catered to a more upscale clientele. There were actually brushstrokes on the restful landscapes above the bed and dresser, and the bathroom even contained a wall-mounted hair dryer. Jenna took a pair of manicure scissors from her bag and spent several minutes cutting her Jenna Kendrick driver's license and credit cards into tiny pieces and flushing them down the toilet. Then she went back out to the rented Plymouth and set off to find the nearest shopping mall.

By two-fifteen that afternoon, her transformation was complete. She had become Susan Devers. She studied her reflection in the mirror on the back of the folding closet door: reddish-brown hair in a sleek, boyishly short cut; face scrubbed clean of makeup; snug, acid-washed jeans; fashionable oversize T-shirt; and pristine white tennis shoes.

Good enough, she decided with a satisfied nod. She lifted a hand to run her fingers through the newly cut fringe of bangs, then had to fight back a sudden swell of tears.

None of that, she told herself resolutely. Not now. She collected the paraphernalia from the box of hair dye and crammed it into a garbage bag that already held her old clothes and the price tags from her new ones, then carried the bag out to a Dumpster bin at the rear of the motel.

Back in the room, she took a small notebook from her purse, sat on the edge of the bed and dialed the first phone number on a short list. Luckily, she found exactly what she was after on the second call. It was a few minutes before three in the afternoon when she locked the door behind her and climbed into the Plymouth. The attendant had given her clear directions over the phone. She shouldn't have any problem finding the George E. Gantner Building, which housed the St. Louis County Morgue and Medical Examiner's Office.

DENNIS BARNES'S FRUSTRATION had reached an intolerable level. The Feds were watching her house, which meant that even if she returned he wouldn't be able to get to her there. And now Verda wasn't available to keep an eye on her at the agency.

He regretted losing his temper with Verda last night, not so much because her injuries would temporarily sideline her, but because he prided himself on his discipline and control. He briefly considered calling his other contact at the Pendergrass agency into service, but quickly dismissed the idea. Allowing Verda to recruit someone so completely unreliable had been one of his rare lapses of judgment.

He calmed himself with the assurance that Jenna couldn't have vanished into thin air. Wherever she was, sooner or later she would need money. Especially if, as he suspected, she'd disassociated herself from the Marshals Service and the Witness Security Program. As soon as she made a withdrawal from her secret savings account, he would have her. He was confident that the Justice Department wasn't aware the account existed. She hadn't *wanted* them to know about it. He would just have to wait for word that she'd presented herself at Nolan Matson's bank.

Meanwhile, he would return to Maryland and show up precisely on time for the appointment with his parole officer. That should ruffle a few feathers at Justice, he thought with a grim smile. And while he was waiting for Jenna to surface, he might as well find out what he could about this writer she'd become involved with.

JENNA DIDN'T HAVE TO pretend to be overwrought for the deputy medical examiner's benefit. This part of the plan had seemed so simple when she'd worked out the details in the comfort and security of her little rented house. But actually transferring her own identity to a dead stranger was turning out to be a lot harder than she'd anticipated.

The legal aspects aside—what she was doing was against the law, and if she was caught there was a good chance she would end up in jail—the "Jane Doe" who was being kept in cold storage somewhere behind those wide stainless-steel doors had been somebody's daughter. Maybe somebody's sister, wife . . . mother.

Jenna had come equipped with what she hoped would be sufficient documentation—several old, slightly out-of-focus photographs of herself, plus records that charted her medical history up to age eighteen.

"I'm sorry I didn't think to bring her dental records, too," she apologized to the deputy M.E. She was shivering, and only partly because the small office she'd been escorted to was so cold.

"If we need them, I'm sure your family dentist will provide them," the young woman replied with a kind smile. The badge on her white lab coat identified her as Laura Spencer. She looked about the same age as Jenna. "You say you've been trying to find your sister—excuse me, your half sister—for about a month?"

Jenna nodded. "That's right. She's taken off like this before, but she never stayed away so long. We—that is, my mother and I—started to worry when she hadn't come home after two weeks." She lowered her gaze to her hands, which were torturing the strap of the cheap plastic purse in her lap. Even though she'd rehearsed this part, she found she couldn't look the other woman in the eye.

"She's been a little...wild, ever since her father died last year. Kendra was always very close to him, and I guess she just couldn't handle..."

The shaking invaded her voice. She stopped, swallowed hard, cleared her throat. How could she do this—sit here and recite this fiction about some poor woman she'd never met?

"Excuse me. This is...difficult. This past month has been..."

"That's quite all right," Laura Spencer murmured. Her tone was as kind and compassionate as her smile. She looked down at the photos and medical records spread across her desk and frowned thoughtfully, as if she was making up her mind about something.

"Dental charts would certainly help authenticate your sister's identity, but I think what you've provided will do." She paused, folding her hands on top of a five-by-seven photo of a twenty-year-old Jenna. "Frankly, Miss Devers, these photographs are enough to convince me, but I'm afraid there's one more thing we have to get out of the way before I can certify that the person we have is in fact Kendra Jenner and release her remains."

Her remains. Every muscle in Jenna's body went rigid. She knew what was coming, and she didn't think she could go through with it.

"We can do this either of two ways," Laura Spencer continued, still in the same gentle voice. "You can come with me into the morgue and identify the body..."

The room began to spin.

"... but I think that in this case, the other method of identification would be best." She opened a manila folder and removed three snapshots. Her tone became even softer, almost apologetic.

"These were taken when she was brought into the morgue. They'll be difficult for you to look at, but trust me, viewing the body would be even worse. She's been here almost three weeks."

Jenna closed her eyes and concentrated on pulling refrigerated, faintly fetid air into her lungs. She vacillated between relief that she'd been given a choice and fear of what the pictures would reveal.

"All right," she heard herself say as she opened her eyes and held out a hand. "If you think this way would be better..."

Laura Spencer passed the snapshots across the desk. Jenna steeled herself, looked down at the first one.

And fainted.

Chapter Eight

The face in the photo might have been her own. Or, more correctly, her younger sister's, if she'd had a younger sister. Now she understood why her own old, blurry photos had been all the evidence Laura Spencer required. The resemblance was uncanny and, at first, terrifying. Even with her face bruised and swollen, Jane Doe had looked more like her than her real sister Kayla had.

When she'd recovered from the shock and completed the necessary paperwork, Jenna was able to perceive the gruesome irony at work, and to be thankful for it. If the deputy medical examiner had harbored any lingering doubts, they were erased when she took one look at the first snapshot and fainted dead away.

As for the woman whose misused and battered corpse was by now on the way to a small mortuary in Jenna's Maryland hometown, she would have a proper burial, complete with a tombstone bearing the name Kendra Jenner. It was the least Jenna could do, and small enough recompense for the new life Jane Doe had given her.

Another new life. Hopefully the last new life, the one that would free her of Dennis Barnes and the United States Department of Justice once and for all. Though, to be honest, she owed Roy Stevenson and his staff a debt of gratitude. Her five-year sojourn in the Witness Security Program had provided a valuable primer for the contingency plan she had formulated in secret.

Except for the visit to the morgue, everything had been remarkably easy. If the general population ever realized just *how* easy, Jenna suspected a lot more people would start dropping out of sight every year.

She'd known from the day she decided to testify against Dennis Barnes that she couldn't entrust her safety to the Marshals Service indefinitely. The federal prosecutor had made it clear that even if Barnes served his entire sentence, which wasn't likely, he would only be imprisoned for fifteen years, max. Jenna had started devising her own private witness protection plan immediately after that conversation, before the trial had even begun.

Anticipating that a new Social Security number would be the first and most important necessity, she'd spent hours at the library, scanning microfiche records of the obituary columns from old newspapers. She finally found the short obituary notice of a girl who had died at the age of three in a rural community. The girl's name was Susan Devers; she'd been born just a few days after Jenna. If Susan had lived, they would be almost exactly the same age. Jenna sent for a certified copy of Susan Devers's birth certificate to make sure they also belonged to the same race. Then she'd reached a dead end, not having any idea how to acquire a phony Social Security number in Susan's name and afraid that if she made a straightforward application she would be found out.

Hopefully Dennis Barnes would never know that it had been one of his former employees who actually procured a legal, bona fide card for Jenna. She had met and befriended the elderly man—a one-time master forger whose failing eyesight had forced him to give up that career—while working as Barnes's secretary. Josef had been happy to help her. She had always suspected that he knew exactly why she wanted a set of false identification.

She'd brought the Social Security card and birth certificate to St. Louis with her. Fortunately, it hadn't been hard to obtain a voter registration card and driver's license in Missouri. Over a two-year period, Susan also applied for and was issued several credit cards. She used the cards judiciously, always making sure to pay for her charges, by money order, within thirty days.

Anyone who bothered to investigate Susan Devers would discover that she was a model citizen who paid her bills on time and had never been issued so much as a parking ticket. Her only fault seemed to be that, like many Americans, she failed to exercise her right to vote.

Susan would miss the Gateway to the West, but it was time to move on. She just wasn't sure where she would go from here.

WHEN THE COMBINED EFFORTS of the FBI and the Marshals Service still hadn't turned up any leads on either Jenna or Dennis Barnes by Saturday morning,

Adam decided to take matters into his own hands. The others could concentrate on locating Barnes; he had to find Jenna.

Either she'd gone into hiding or Barnes had found her. But if Barnes had found her, he should have returned to Maryland. Adam would have denied it to his superiors, but he hoped Dennis Barnes stayed missing for a while yet.

He started hitting small, out-of-the-way motels early Saturday morning. It didn't occur to him until he'd struck out eight times that Jenna might have registered under another name.

JENNA FINISHED PACKING her new clothes and then took a few minutes to inspect the room. After all her careful planning, it would be stupid to leave something behind that could be used to identify her.

Satisfied that she hadn't overlooked anything, she carried the tan vinyl suitcase to the rented Plymouth and drove around to the motel office to check out. Adam, Jr., gazed at her from the passenger seat. His soft plush coat was a little damp from the tears he'd absorbed the night before. Jenna didn't know why she still had the basset hound. She should have tossed him into the Dumpster out back. Heaven knew she didn't want any reminders of Adam Case or his deceit and betrayal. But the stuffed dog was company, of sorts. Better than nothing, anyway, she told herself, giving his head an affectionate pat as she switched off the engine.

She was tucking her Susan Devers credit card back into her wallet as she turned from the checkout desk, so she didn't see the 1966 Tahoe Turquoise Mustang pull up to the curb or the tall, lean man in faded jeans and cowboy boots climb out and hurry around the car. She was halfway across the lobby before she looked up, to find Adam just outside, walking straight toward her.

He grabbed the handle of the plate-glass door and yanked it open. For one panic-stricken moment Jenna's heart stopped. She forgot how to breathe. And then he was inside, no more than twenty feet away. Reacting purely on impulse, she swerved toward a rack of tourism brochures at one side of the small lobby.

He walked right past her, didn't even glance in her direction. Jenna selected a couple of colorful pamphlets at random and forced herself to casually stroll out the door and across the pavement to the rented car. Heart pounding, she locked herself inside and fumbled in her purse for the keys. She couldn't find them. She hadn't left them on the checkout desk, had she?

She swiveled to empty the purse on the passenger seat and spotted the basset hound an instant before she saw Adam shove back through the lobby door. His fierce scowl dimmed her relief when her searching fingers finally located the car keys. She'd never seen anything approaching that expression on his face. He looked and moved like a man possessed as his long legs carried him around the Mustang.

Jenna ducked her head slightly and nudged the dog onto the floor, in case he should glance in her direction. He didn't. If there'd been a cop around, he probably would have gotten a ticket for reckless driving when he pulled out of the motel driveway.

She sat in the car for several minutes, until she got some control over her emotions. After what she'd heard in Roy Stevenson's office, the sight of Adam should have filled her with rage and loathing. He was a hypocritical, manipulative, unscrupulous bastard. She should hate him; she *wanted* to hate him. So why did just looking at him hurt so damned much?

What had he been doing at this motel? she wondered as she lifted his namesake back onto the seat and started the car. Was he looking for her? The thought triggered a flare of hope that enraged her. *Fool!* she told herself scathingly. If he is looking for you, it's only because he wants to take you into custody—or use you again, probably as bait to catch Dennis Barnes.

The reminder stiffened her spine and her resolve. From now on, Adam Case and the rest of his Justice Department cronies would have to earn their salaries without her help. She had one more stop to make, and then she would leave the lot of them behind, for good.

JENNA HAD SELECTED the bank because, in their eagerness to attract local customers, the board of directors had decided to keep several suburban branches open for business on Saturday and Sunday. When the time came, she knew she would need immediate access to the savings account she'd established shortly after arriving in St. Louis.

No one outside the bank knew about the account, or that it had been opened with a check from her sister, Kayla—the last present Kayla had given her, a thank-you for enabling her to finally escape her abusive marriage to Dennis Barnes. At the time, neither of them had known what her new name would be.

Consequently, both the check and the savings account bore the name Kendra Jenner.

By now the account held an impressive balance. Having anticipated the bank officers' reluctance to hand over so much money in a lump sum, Jenna asked for several certified checks payable to the bearer, which she would use to open another account wherever she finally settled, and the balance in cash. Closing the account still took an exasperatingly long amount of time. She was anxious to be on the road, to put St. Louis and the people who were looking for her—*all* the people who were looking for her—as far behind her as possible, as quickly as possible.

DENNIS BARNES RECEIVED Nolan Matson's phone call at a little before one in the afternoon. Barnes had returned home early that morning, hidden in the back of a van belonging to the landscaping firm that routinely serviced the grounds of his estate. He interrupted his lunch to take the banker's call.

"She's here!" Matson said excitedly. "Right now, closing out the account! I can see her from my office. She's changed her looks—cut and dyed her hair—but it's her. She had the necessary ID, and her signature matches the one on file."

Barnes suppressed the rush of triumph that surged inside him, reminding himself that she was still a thousand miles away and he could lose her again when she left Matson's bank.

"Call Frank," he said curtly. "Now. Tell him to get over there on the double and follow her when she leaves."

"Frank?" Matson sounded dubious. "What if she spots him?"

"He'll only have to stay with her for an hour or so, until I can get one of my people into place." Barnes paused briefly, then added, "Tell him if he manages not to screw up, all debts will be canceled."

"Good thinking," Matson observed. "That should motivate him."

After he hung up, Barnes stood for a minute at the window wall that overlooked sprawling, manicured lawns, a pool, guest house and, at the rear of the property, an enormous air-conditioned stable that housed two strings of polo ponies. At the moment, the physical confirmation of his wealth meant nothing. He'd have traded it all to be outside Matson's bank when she came out. Unfortunately, even if that were possible, he knew he didn't dare leave again so soon.

Patience, he counseled himself. The important thing was not to lose her again. Who to send, to follow and watch her? One name came to mind: Ross. He turned back to the telephone and punched a button that automatically dialed a number stored in memory.

SATURDAY NIGHT of a three-day holiday weekend. The emergency rooms of every hospital within fifty miles were filled to capacity, mostly with drunk drivers and their victims.

Adam sat in front of Roy Stevenson's desk, eyes closed, head resting against the back of the chair. His head hadn't touched a pillow since Thursday night, and he wasn't sleeping now. Nor did he expect to anytime soon. His body was exhausted, but his mind was like a rat on one of those squeaky wire wheels, racing frantically and getting absolutely nowhere.

He'd given up on the motels late in the afternoon, finally conceding that he was wasting precious time. The local law-enforcement teams would start from scratch on Monday—or more likely Tuesday, since they'd probably have their hands full till then. Each officer would be provided with a two-year-old file photo of Jenna, something he would have thought to take with him that morning, if he'd been thinking.

Roy had already checked with Jenna's bank when he returned to the office. Her checking and savings accounts were still intact: no large withdrawals or transfers. Adam wasn't encouraged by the news. If she was on the run, or even hiding out somewhere in the area, she'd need cash. He didn't think she would use her credit cards. She'd know the charges would be easy to trace.

On the other hand, she might also be aware that because it was a long weekend and most businesses had just forwarded their charge slips for the preceding month, they would probably hold new slips for several days. So she *might* be using the credit cards for purchases or cash advances.

The key to finding her was to think like she did, try to anticipate what she would do before she did it. Usually Adam was good at that, especially when he'd had time to study the other person's habits and character. He had a knack for putting himself inside his subject's skin, examining the situation from his or her perspective and, almost always, accurately predicting how the subject would behave.

But not this time. The irony didn't escape him. It should have been easier this time. His "subject" was the woman he loved. In some ways he'd come to know her better, more intimately, in the past week and a half than he'd ever known anyone. And yet there was so much of her he didn't know, so much she'd kept hidden—secret, scarred regions of her heart and mind that she hadn't trusted him enough to expose.

He wanted to know all those places. He ached with the need to have her bare them to him, willingly, to give him the chance to heal them. And he was terrified that he would never have that chance.

He prayed that she *was* hiding somewhere. From Barnes, or from him, or from both of them, he didn't care. *Please, God,* he asked as he stared at the ceiling of Roy Stevenson's office, *just keep her safe. And let me find her before he does.*

JENNA STOPPED for the night at a small, ten-unit motel on I-70, about halfway between Vandalia and Effingham, Illinois. After checking in, she took the car to a gas station across the road to fill up the tank. When she went inside to pay for the gas, she bought a road atlas from a stack next to the cash register.

"Startin' a trip?" the teenager behind the counter asked as he returned her Susan Devers charge card.

"Yes," Jenna replied with a smile. "I'm heading up to Chicago."

At least, that was what she wanted anyone who might pick up her trail to think, which was why she'd used the credit card. She had no intention of going anywhere near Chicago. Dennis Barnes had too many "associates" there. She needed to find someplace off the beaten path, someplace so far out of the way that neither Barnes nor the bureaucrats from the Justice Department would think of looking for her there.

She would study the atlas tonight, she decided over dinner at a truck stop next to the gas station. She had enough cash to stay on the move for weeks, maybe months, but she had no intention of spending the rest of her life running and hiding.

ADAM FELT SHELL-SHOCKED. After two days without even the thinnest, most improbable suggestion of a lead, the blows had fallen so fast that he hadn't had time to absorb the impact of one before the next one hit.

First Jenna's Escort had been discovered Sunday morning, apparently abandoned, in a downtown parking garage. He was still trying to decide whether she'd intentionally left it there when Roy received word that Dennis Barnes was back at his Maryland estate, receiving a steady stream of visitors.

"Doesn't look good," Roy muttered, giving voice to thoughts Adam didn't dare speak aloud.

But the worst was yet to come. When they'd had no success canvassing area hospitals, Roy had pulled Marvin Bolander from Jenna's house and dispatched him to the St. Louis County Morgue. Roy was on another line when Marv phoned in. Adam picked up the call at the secretary's desk, which he'd taken over for the remainder of the weekend.

"Looks like we've found her," Marv said without preamble.

Adam's stomach heaved as if the entire building had suddenly dropped fifty feet.

"Tell me," he said in a hollow voice.

"A Jane Doe was identified as Kendra Jenner on Friday afternoon and shipped out to Maryland yesterday morning."

GORDON ROSS HAD TAKEN over and sent Frank Pendergrass back to St. Louis when the woman pulled off the interstate northeast of Vandalia.

Ross had been aboard Dennis Barnes's private jet, en route from Chicago to Memphis, when Barnes reached him. Fifteen minutes later the plane landed at the Mount Vernon, Illinois, airport, where Ross transferred to a waiting car. After that he was in almost constant contact with Frank over the cellular phone, so he knew exactly when and where she left the interstate and which motel she'd checked into for the night.

Like shooting fish in a barrel, Ross thought as he let himself into the room next to hers. She's already between the cross hairs, and she doesn't have a clue. He unpacked only what he'd need for the night, then sat on the double bed, and placed a person-to-person call to Maryland.

The next day, Sunday, he followed her northeast to the I-57 interchange, where she unexpectedly turned south. Hell, Ross thought, Barnes should have let me go on to Memphis. Unless she made another course change, that was where she was headed. She didn't appear to be in any hurry, though. She stayed at or under the speed limit, made several short rest stops and pulled off the interstate again just north of Mount Vernon. Ross snorted in disgust as he lugged a khaki duffel bag to his room. They were within three or four miles of the airport where he'd made the unscheduled stop the day before.

"WHAT ARE THE CHANCES it was a mistaken ID?"

It was Roy who asked. He'd picked up the extension in his office just as Marv delivered his devastating message, and it was good that he had. Adam knew better than to try to speak just yet. Listening was causing him enough agony. He wondered if he was having a heart attack, almost hoped he was. Would that be adequate punishment for his sins?

"Slim to none, I'd say," Marv replied glumly. "It was her sister who identified her."

"Her *sister!*"

Roy's voice exploded in Adam's ear, making him flinch but at the same time liberating him from the pain that had been threatening to strangle him.

"Her sister." Adam repeated the words in a low, cautious tone, afraid to even breathe lest he extinguish the spark of hope that had flickered to life inside him. "How many sisters did she have?"

"One," Roy said flatly. "Kayla Jenner Barnes."

"Uh-uh," Marv muttered. "That's not the name this woman gave. Just a sec." There was a pause, during which Adam and Roy heard the faint rustle of paper. "Here it is—Susan Devers. And an address in Granite City."

"Do you think—" Adam swiveled toward Roy's office, met the marshal's perplexed gaze through the open door. "Is it possible Kayla didn't die in the plane crash? Could she be enrolled in the Witness Security Program, too?"

Roy shook his head adamantly. "No way. If she lives in Granite City, she'd be under the protection of this office."

Marv hesitantly suggested another possibility. "But could she still be alive? Faked her own death, maybe, and assumed a new identity to keep Barnes from coming after her and their son?"

"Sure, and they've been living in Granite City, Illinois, for the past five years," Roy scoffed, but Adam heard the trace of uncertainty in his voice.

"How hard would it be to check?"

"On a holiday weekend?"

"So we hassle a few people at home," Marv put in. "I think it's worth looking into. I can start by driving over to Granite City tonight, see if the address she gave checks out."

"Meanwhile I'll make a few calls to Washington," Adam added. The spark had grown to a tiny, fragile flame. "I'll try to find out if there was any question about Kayla and Thad Barnes's identification after the plane crash."

Roy didn't object to their plans, but, from the outer office, Adam felt the weight of his doubt. It was almost enough to snuff out the flickering flame of hope. Almost. If Susan Devers *was* Kayla Barnes, she could be helping her sister to disappear the same way she herself had five years ago.

He made his calls and was told it would be the next day before anyone could get into the Barnes files. Rather than sit around waiting for Marv to report in, he decided to go to Jenna's house. Maybe she'd left something, some clue about where she'd been headed.

There was nothing. Except for the open overnight case on the bed, the house looked exactly as it had when he'd practically forced her to leave Thursday night. As far as he could tell, she hadn't even taken any clothes. Her toothbrush was back in the bathroom; a single plate and wine glass rested in the drying rack next to the double sink. His uneaten half of the pizza sat in the refrigerator.

He wandered back into the bedroom, his hope fading fast. There was nothing here to suggest that she'd planned to be gone more than a few hours. She hadn't taken anything with her, not even her cosmetics. A collection of bottles, jars and tubes sat on the dresser, along with an imitation tortoiseshell comb-and-brush set.

He stubbornly resisted the obvious conclusion, that she'd intended to come back. He was missing something. It was right here, staring him in the face. He just wasn't seeing it. A faint rectangular mark on the carpet next to the bed caught his eye and he knelt to examine it. On closer inspection he saw that it wasn't a stain, as he'd first thought, just an area where the nap had been squashed by something heavy.

He leaned down, peering under the bed, and found a large, flat plastic box. When he pulled it out, it perfectly covered the flattened area of carpet. The box contained stacks of neatly folded sweaters, obviously stored there for the summer, and below them he discovered the cast-aluminum document safe they'd been arranged to conceal.

Adam sat back on his heels and stared at the safe. What kinds of papers would Jenna keep hidden under her bed in a safe with a combination lock?

IT WAS THE PAMPHLETS she grabbed back at the motel in St. Louis, when she'd been dodging Adam, that gave her the idea. One of them was a six-page, full-color brochure for the Shawnee National Forest area in the tip of southern Illinois. According to the brochure, the entire area was as close to undeveloped wilderness as she was likely to find in this part of the country. It sounded like the perfect place to lose herself for a while.

Chapter Nine

Adam and Roy were waiting when Laura Spencer arrived at the morgue Monday morning.

The young deputy M.E. hadn't been on duty when Marv was there the night before, so Roy spent a few minutes briefing her about Kendra and Kayla Jenner. Adam waited in taut, anxious silence, slouched on an institutional gray metal chair, trying to ignore the smell that permeated every surface of the building. These places always gave him the creeps, and this time was worse than usual.

"Let's see if I understand," Laura Spencer murmured when Roy finished. "You think the woman who presented herself as Susan Devers may actually have been Kayla Jenner Barnes, who was supposed to have died in a plane crash five years ago."

"You got it," Roy said brusquely. Adam had the feeling that he, too, would have preferred to be anywhere else.

"She had a driver's license and credit cards that identified her as Susan Devers."

Roy shrugged. "It wouldn't be the first time somebody used fake ID."

"I guess not," Laura muttered. She was clearly skeptical, unwilling to believe she might have been taken in. "But she was very convincing. Upset, worried . . . wanting to find out what had happened to her sister, but at the same time afraid of finding out. Of course, she'd put off checking with us until she'd exhausted every other possibility. That's typical. She said she'd been looking for her sister for a month."

Adam abruptly sat up straight. "A month?"

Laura nodded. "That's right. She was visibly distraught, as you can imagine. I didn't question her story for a second, especially since they *looked* so much alike."

Roy turned to Adam to remark, "We should've brought a file photo."

Laura snapped her fingers. "Photos—of course! I've got two sets—the pictures we took when the Jane Doe came in, and some Susan Devers brought of her sister."

Both men leaned forward expectantly as she lifted a stack of manila folders from the out basket on a corner of her desk.

"The file should still be here," she murmured, shuffling through the folders. "Most of the staff has the weekend off. Yes, here it is."

She spread the photos out for them to examine.

"She might have been lying about her name, but I'd be willing to bet the Jane Doe really was her sister," she said. "The poor woman took one look at the photos and passed out cold."

Adam concentrated on breathing deeply, through his mouth, so he wouldn't do the same.

"Damn," Roy said softly.

They were both thinking it. Adam said it aloud, his voice raw, as he picked up a five-by-seven photo of Jenna. "It's her."

"You see," Laura Spencer said, sounding vindicated. "I knew as soon as Susan Devers or Kayla Barnes or whatever her name is walked in that she had to be a relative." She lifted several papers that had been stapled together, scanning the first couple of pages as she continued.

"Even if she hadn't brought her sister's medical records—" She suddenly broke off. "Oh, no. This can't be."

Adam barely registered Roy's sharp "What?" as the marshal half rose from his chair to see what she was reading, but her anxious response captured his complete attention.

"There's no record of an appendectomy."

Warmth began to seep back into Adam's body. "She doesn't have a scar," he said, unconsciously using the present tense.

"Yes, she did," Laura insisted, holding up another set of papers. "It's right here, under scars, birthmarks, et cetera. Our Jane Doe definitely had an appendectomy scar!"

"But Jenna Kendrick doesn't," he countered.

Her forehead puckered in a baffled frown. "Who?"

"Kendra Jenner," Roy supplied. Swiveling to face Adam, he demanded, "You're sure?"

"Positive." He wondered if the immense relief he was feeling showed on his face, then decided he didn't give a damn if it did. He studied the photo in his hand, eyes narrowed in concentration.

"I think," he said slowly, working it out as he spoke, "we should forget the Jane Doe for now and focus on Susan Devers."

He turned the photo toward Roy, his certainty growing as stunned comprehension replaced the other man's dubious frown.

"Son of a gun," Roy breathed.

The deputy M.E. was staring at them as if they'd suddenly started speaking a foreign language.

"*This* is Kendra Jenner," Adam said, flipping the photo across the desk at her. "Or rather, *was* Kendra Jenner, in a former life. For the past five years she's been Jenna Kendrick. And then sometime last Friday she apparently turned herself into Susan Devers."

Laura glanced down at the photo, then back at him. "Who did we send to Maryland?" she asked, aghast.

AN HOUR AND A HALF LATER, Adam was back at Jenna's house. He'd come to retrieve the document safe under her bed. Not that he expected they'd find anything in it. No doubt that was where she'd stashed her Susan Devers ID.

He found a clean pillowcase in the tiny linen closet and carefully slipped it around the safe before lifting it onto the bed. Then he sat down beside it and rubbed a hand over bleary, burning eyes. The face that glared back at him from the mirror above the dresser might have belonged to a derelict or a psychopath—haggard and grim, with a two-day growth of beard and a thin-lipped, red-eyed stare that would have frightened children and most sensible adults.

His brain felt fried. He'd been running mostly on adrenaline and caffeine since Friday afternoon. Remembering the pizza in the fridge, he got up and made his way to the kitchen. As he waited for the microwave to finish heating the pizza, he was again seized by the conviction that he was missing something—something here, in the house. But what, dammit? Not the safe; something else. Something she'd taken, or maybe neglected to take.

The microwave timer went off a second before he heard the front door open and close. He automatically tensed.

"Adam?" Roy's voice called from the living room.

Adam closed his eyes and expelled a disappointed sigh. "In the kitchen." He was sitting down with the pizza when Roy entered the room. "Join me?"

Roy shook his head and slid into the chair across from him. He didn't seem at all surprised to find Adam fixing himself lunch in Jenna's kitchen. "No, thanks. There's news—both kinds. Take your pick."

"Good," Adam said around a mouthful of pizza. He didn't think he could handle any more bad news until he'd got some food in his stomach.

Roy stuck his thumb in the air. "One. Kayla Barnes's body was positively identified after the plane crash. They used her dental records. Which means she definitely isn't Susan Devers."

Adam nodded and kept eating.

"Two." Roy extended his index finger alongside the thumb. "Jane Doe arrived at the funeral home in Maryland this morning. I had the sheriff's department send somebody over to fingerprint the corpse. Whoever she was, she wasn't Jenna. The FBI is running the prints now. Hopefully they'll get a match and an ID."

Adam washed down a mouthful of pizza with a swallow of apple juice and said nothing. This was only confirmation of what they'd already known. Before they left the morgue, Laura Spencer had informed them that the Jane Doe had been a three-week resident.

"Three." Roy's middle finger joined the other two digits. "Our eager-beaver rookie marshal took it upon himself to check the few banks in the area that stayed open for business during the weekend. He didn't turn up any new accounts in Jenna's name, but he *did* find a savings account under the name Kendra Jenner that was closed out on Saturday morning."

Adam absorbed the information with a frown. "So she has money." He didn't know whether to be relieved that she wasn't penniless and hungry, or discouraged—ready cash would make it easier for her to hide.

"Several thousand," Roy confirmed. "Enough to take her just about anywhere. She'd been making deposits regularly for five years. The local police started checking motels about a half hour ago. I gave them all three names, along with the file photo, but it may be a while before we get any results. That's it for the good news."

Adam leaned back in his chair. "Okay, let's have the bad."

"The FBI finally provided us with a list of Dennis Barnes's known associates in the area, and the president of the bank where she had the Kendra Jenner account is right up near the top."

The pizza and apple juice roiled in Adam's stomach. "So Barnes was probably tipped off as soon as she closed the account."

"More than likely," Roy agreed. "He may even have had her followed. But at least he's still in Maryland, or was, as of eleven-thirty this morning. His parole hearing's tomorrow, so even if he does know where she is, I doubt he'll go after her before then."

Adam's flat stare was blatantly disbelieving.

"I'm trying to be positive here. Look on the bright side," Roy muttered.

Adam didn't reply. So far as he could see, there wasn't any bright side. Jenna was alive, but God knew for how much longer. She was running, deliberately hiding, from the people who'd been assigned to protect her, as well as from Dennis Barnes. They didn't have a clue where to start looking for her, while Barnes had probably been aware of every move she made since she'd closed out the Kendra Jenner bank account last Saturday.

He thought that if she should suddenly walk through the front door, he would probably grab her and shake her till her teeth rattled. Or grab her and just hold her. And kiss her deaf, dumb and blind. And then fall down on his knees and beg her to forgive him.

JENNA PASSED THROUGH Harrisburg, Equality and Horseshoe, and finally stopped at a wide spot in the road called Utopia. An appropriate appellation, she supposed, since the place was within a stone's throw of the area of the Shawnee National Forest known as the Garden of the Gods.

Utopia's main drag boasted a dry goods-video rental store cum gas station, a couple of cafés, a small brick building shared by a general practitioner and a dentist, several stores and some houses and the five-unit Utopia Motor Inn.

By 1:00 p.m. Monday, Jenna had settled into one of the motor inn's three vacant cabins and set off for a walking tour of the town. By one-thirty, she'd seen pretty much all there was to see—enough, at any rate, to persuade her that this would be a good place to disappear for a while. Not only was it off the beaten path, the scenery was gorgeous, the air was crisp and crystal clear, and the people were polite and friendly.

One, an attractive man in a deputy sheriff's uniform, had been a shade too friendly for her comfort. She'd run into him, literally, on the sidewalk in front of one of the cafés. He'd been on his way out, settling his hat on his head, and neither of them had seen the other until it was too late to avoid a collision.

"Pardon me, ma'am!" he'd exclaimed, reaching out to steady her with one hand while the other instinctively flew up to touch the brim of his buff Stetson. Great, she'd thought. Another John Law cowboy type. It must be her karma to keep encountering them at greasy spoons.

"My fault entirely," he said. His smile exposed a mouthful of gleaming white teeth. "You okay, ma'am?"

Jenna had assured him she was fine, no damage done, and ducked into the café. But when she slid into one of the front booths and glanced over the top of the menu, she saw him through the window, still standing on the sidewalk, watching her with an appreciative glint in his eyes. He ducked his head, flashed another smile and touched his hat again before ambling off in the direction of the post office.

Jenna watched him go. He was incredibly handsome, she had to admit. He'd be making big bucks as an actor or model if he lived in New York or Los Angeles. But there was a cockiness in his smile and loose-limbed swagger that turned her off—a self-confidence that verged on arrogance. He probably never passed a reflective surface without practicing that killer smile.

She found herself comparing the deputy's obvious conceit to Adam's casual, effortless charm. Her hand clenched, crumpling the edge of the menu. Right, she thought bitterly as she laid the laminated sheet of cardboard on the table and attempted to press out the crease she'd made. He was charming, all right—because he'd figured that would be the fastest, easiest way to get what he wanted.

Without warning, the reproach she'd overheard Roy Stevenson toss at him rang through her mind: *"You're dead wrong about her, always have been. She didn't conspire with Barnes to secure the lesser charges."*

Always have been.

And there had been more. What else had Roy said? Something about the government's having thrown away the case Adam had built five years ago.

How long had he been planning and scheming, before he strolled into the Pendergrass agency and leveled that warm, lazy drawl and irresistible smile at her? Before he set out to wine and dine her and sweep her off her feet?

"I'm new in town and feeling lonely as an orphaned hound dog...."

"He's housebroken and low-maintenance. (So am I, by the way.)"

A giant fist squeezed her heart. Tears stung her eyes. Jenna angrily dashed them away. Damn him! The deceitful, two-faced fraud! But then other phrases penetrated her pain and anger, whispering slyly in her ear, raising doubts and unwanted hopes.

"I didn't mean for this to happen." "Remember this. When everything's gone to hell and you despise us both ... remember."

"There are things I have to tell you...."

Had he intended to tell her who he was that last night—the night Dennis Barnes came after her? She'd have given anything to believe that he had; that making love with her hadn't just been part of his master plan; that he cared enough to want to start over, with no lies or secrets between them. She wanted desperately to believe it, but she didn't dare. She'd burned all her bridges. It wasn't just her broken heart at stake now, but her life.

A loud commotion from the direction of the kitchen brought her attention back to her immediate surroundings. A minute later, a balding man wearing a stained apron hustled a middle-aged woman through a set of swinging doors and across the café dining room. A clean white dishtowel was wrapped around the woman's right arm. She was deathly pale, her lips pressed together in pain. A younger woman followed them into the dining room. The dozen or so customers watched the drama with interest, but no one offered assistance.

"Call Doc Mitchell," the man yelled over his shoulder. "Tell 'im we're on the way."

The younger woman made for the phone on the counter beside the cash register as they reached the café entrance. When she'd completed the call, she put a hand to her chest, heaved an eloquent sigh, then glanced up and noticed Jenna. Pulling an order pad from the pocket of her apron, she hurried over to the booth.

"Sorry for the delay," she said as she plucked a pencil from above her right ear. "We were already shorthanded, and now this."

"Was she burned?" Jenna asked.

The waitress nodded brusquely. "It's that old stove. Eb should've replaced it years ago. Whole thing's cast-iron. The oven door weighs a ton and gets hotter than Hades. It fell on Nora's arm just as she was gettin' ready to take out some pies. Are you ready to order, or do you need some more time to study the menu?"

"I'll order now," Jenna said. There wasn't that much to study. "I'll have a cheeseburger, medium rare, a salad with Thousand Island dressing and a glass of ice tea. No lemon."

When the waitress finished scribbling the order on her pad, she pointed out that the burger would take a while since she'd have to fry it herself. Jenna said that was fine, she was in no hurry. Apparently the salads were already made up, because hers was in front of her, along with a tall glass of ice tea, within two minutes. The balding cook, who she assumed was also the café's owner, returned a few minutes later, just after the waitress had placed a half-cooked cheeseburger on a soggy bun in front of her. The poor man looked as if one more crisis would finish him off. Making an impulsive decision, Jenna slid out of the booth and walked over to him before she could change her mind.

"Excuse me, sir," she said politely. "I couldn't help noticing that you're a little shorthanded, and since I happen to need a job—"

He didn't let her finish. "You're hired. Pay's minimum wage, plus tips. Go grab an apron and an order pad from the kitchen. Tillie will show you where."

GORDON ROSS LOOKED like most of the people who visited the area to spend a day or two hiking, rock climbing, horseback riding and communing with nature before they got back on the interstate and rejoined the rat race. When he appeared on Utopia's main street—stopping at the grocery store to stock his ice chest or the gas station to top off the tank of his Jeep—he wore faded walking shorts, a T-shirt and scuffed hiking boots, and he never left his cabin at the Utopia Motor Inn without a camera slung around his neck. Fortunately everything except the ice chest had been packed in his duffel; he'd been planning to do some white-water rafting in Arkansas once he finished Barnes's business in Memphis. He'd picked up the cheap plastic cooler at a convenience store in Harrisburg.

By Tuesday afternoon he was bored out of his skull. Maybe he could tell Barnes that the woman had noticed him, was beginning to get suspicious, so Barnes would rotate somebody else in to watch her. It wasn't true, of course—Ross had been careful not to call attention to himself, going so far as to change cars at Mount Vernon Sunday evening—but Barnes couldn't know that.

Then again, Barnes had a talent for knowing things he couldn't possibly know, so maybe he should just sit tight and do what he was being paid to do: watch her. Not that she was doing anything worth reporting. She'd apparently decided to stay in the boondocks for a while. By Tuesday morning she'd landed a waitress job and moved into a two-room furnished apartment a block from the restaurant. The apartment was owned by her boss, one Eb Gebhardt, a taciturn man whose only addiction seemed to be to hard work.

Ross decided to have lunch at Eb's Café, in case Barnes asked him about the woman's co-workers. He probably would. He seemed obsessed with everything about her.

ADAM SAT IN ROY'S OFFICE, going over a stack of reports from various sources. The more he read, the more frustrated he became.

Susan Devers had registered at two motels, miles apart, on Friday. She'd spent the night in one and checked out Saturday morning. The discovery that the motel was one of those he'd checked himself didn't improve his mood. He'd probably missed her by no more than an hour or two.

They knew that Jenna was driving a white Plymouth she'd rented as Susan Devers, and that by Saturday evening she'd been halfway across Illinois, apparently headed for Chicago. That last information had been supplied by the employee of a gas station she'd stopped at on I-70, before she'd disappeared again.

Of course, she hadn't really disappeared, Adam reminded himself; they just hadn't located any more of

Susan Devers's credit card charges. Unless she'd switched to using cash, or had another persona no one knew about, "Susan" would turn up again. But where? And how long would it take?

Adam was certain that Dennis Barnes knew exactly where Jenna was, probably had someone watching her at that very moment. Unlike Barnes, he and Roy had limited resources. If they concentrated on the Chicago area, they might be looking in the wrong place when she surfaced again. Meanwhile Barnes would make the meeting with his parole officer this afternoon and then be free to go after her. The FBI and DEA had him under surveillance, but he'd managed to slip away from both agencies before and Adam didn't doubt for a minute that he could do it again.

He sat back and rolled his head to relieve the tension in his neck and shoulders. The past twelve hours hadn't produced anything that would be of immediate use. As he'd expected, the document safe had been empty. The only prints on it were his and Jenna's. Roy and his staff had things under control here. There was nothing for him to do but sit and wait. Adam had never been very good at either. He dashed off a note for Roy that he'd be at Jenna's house, then left.

He tried to shrug off the impression of abandonment he got when he walked through the front door, the sense that the woman who'd lived in this house wasn't coming back. It was just nerves, he told himself. Plus a healthy amount of anxiety, and more than a little guilt. He'd been suppressing the guilt for four days now, trying to deny its existence. He hadn't been very successful. It had damn near overwhelmed him when he first realized Jenna had overheard him talking to Roy about her, and again in that stuffy office at the morgue. It was pressing in on him now.

He closed his eyes and forced himself to concentrate on what he knew, instead of what he felt. She must have been working on her escape plan for a long time, maybe years, but she hadn't implemented it right away. She'd been thinking about bolting Thursday night, when he sensed that she was planning something. But she hadn't. She'd waited, gone to see Roy. Needing and expecting help. Instead, she discovered that she'd been betrayed.

Adam gave up, let the guilt have its way as he wandered aimlessly through the house. There was no reason for him to be here, and he didn't have the slightest idea what he was looking for. She'd planned well. She hadn't taken a damned thing—at least, nothing that would be missed. He gravitated to the bedroom, checked the closet and chest of drawers again. Came up with zip. Again. Dropping down on the bed, he raked both hands through his hair. His reflection seemed to condemn him from the dresser mirror.

You shouldn't have made love to her. Right. He shouldn't have, but he had and he didn't regret it. How could he? That night had been a revelation. He'd never known two people could come so close to merging into a single being. And not just physically, but on every level. He hadn't lied when he told her the experience had knocked him for a loop. He'd been shocked, stunned, dazed. And for an hour or so after she fell asleep, absolutely terrified by the idea of facing her in the morning.

So you ran like the coward you are, rather than stay and tell her the truth. Adam rubbed a hand over his face. Guilty as charged. He'd blown his chance—probably the only chance he would ever have, even if he managed to find her and get to her before Barnes did. After what she'd heard in Roy's office, she must hate his guts. It didn't matter, though. She could curse every breath he drew for the rest of her life. All that mattered was that she *had* a life.

He pushed himself off the bed and glanced around the room one last time. Nothing. Not a clue about what her plans had been or where she was headed. She hadn't even taken her comb and brush....

He froze. The basset hound. He remembered tossing it onto the dresser Wednesday night. It wasn't there, or on the bed. A slow smile spread over his face, softening the harsh lines that had been etched by the grueling past four days.

She'd taken Adam, Jr.

Chapter Ten

The apartment wasn't much to look at: a tiny galley kitchen and a fifteen-by-fifteen foot space that served as living room during the day and bedroom when the couch was opened up at night. An antique air conditioner roosted in the single window, laboring noisily. The bathroom was about the same size as the kitchen and contained a huge old enameled iron bathtub that squatted on claw-and-ball feet.

Cozy, Jenna thought with a wry smile as she carried in a bag of groceries Wednesday morning. There was even a television—a thirteen-inch black-and-white, no cable—and a stereo system, complete with a box of old albums and another of cassette tapes. Not exactly the Ritz, or even the YWCA, but a hundred times better than a motel that would require some kind of identification and probably the number of her license plate.

She put away the groceries—mostly staples, since Eb had agreed to furnish her meals in return for her working double shifts until Nora could come back—opened a can of diet cola and sank down on the couch with Adam, Jr. Things were working out much better than she'd dared hope. She had a job, a place to live, and—as far as she knew—no one had tracked her this far. For a while, back on the interstate, she'd been concerned about a green Firebird she'd noticed shortly after she turned south at Effingham. The car had stayed with her all the way to Mount Vernon, but there was no sign of it when she got back on the road Monday morning.

Remembering the Firebird led her to thinking about Tillie's sales pitch yesterday afternoon, while they were refilling napkin containers and catsup bottles. The other waitress had a '77 Mercury Monarch her son had driven since he got his license. Tillie and her husband wanted to sell the car and get the boy something more economical before he went off to college next year. She swore the Monarch was in tip-top shape, with low mileage and good tires, but the V-8 engine was a real gas guzzler. She was asking a thousand dollars. Jenna suspected she could buy the car for several hundred less. The question was, should she?

She decided she might as well. She couldn't keep the rented Plymouth indefinitely, though she was a little apprehensive about turning it in. She wasn't even sure where the nearest rental-agency office was located. Harrisburg, maybe; it was the last town of any size she'd passed through. Eb would probably know. If he didn't, the deputy would, though after last night she was reluctant to even talk to him, except to take his order.

His name was Jesse Herron, and by Tuesday evening it was clear that her initial impression of him had been right on the mark. He saw himself as God's gift to the female sex. He was supposed to patrol the southern half of Saline County, but he always managed to be in the vicinity of Eb's Café at mealtime. Jesse had been delighted to find Jenna working there when he stopped in at noon yesterday. He'd immediately tried to strike up a conversation, though thankfully he seemed more interested in dazzling her with his movie-star looks and law-enforcement vocabulary than in eliciting personal information from her.

She'd been polite, but reserved. Fortunately, lunch hour had been busy, so she hadn't had to find excuses to avoid him. Unfortunately, the dinner crowd was only about half as large, and most of the customers lingered to exchange local news and gossip over coffee after finishing their meals. Except for shuttling plates and flatware to the kitchen and keeping cups filled, she hadn't had much to do.

Jesse had parked himself at a table near the kitchen and done his best to monopolize her attention for an hour and a half, during which time he drank enough coffee to float a battleship. She sensed that her immunity to his macho magnetism was making him curious. Or maybe he took it as a personal challenge. He didn't budge until the last four customers had filed out the door. Jenna stood behind the cash register and rang up his bill, thinking the man must have cast-iron kidneys.

"So, do you work tomorrow afternoon?" he asked as she counted out his change.

"Yes." Her smile was consciously lackluster. "Two shifts. Nora will be off for several more days."

"Too bad." He stuffed bills into a brown leather wallet with crossed Colt revolvers embossed on the outside. "I was hoping you'd let me show you some of the local scenery. Maybe another time."

"Maybe," Jenna had reluctantly replied.

Now it was almost time to start the first of today's back-to-back shifts. She dreaded walking the block to the café, because she knew Deputy Herron would be there for lunch. She didn't know how long she'd be able to parry his overtures. As she nestled Adam, Jr., into a corner of the couch, she decided to buy the car from Tillie today and find out where she should go to turn in the rental. Then if she had to leave town in a hurry, she'd be ready.

"IS SHE PLANNING to *buy* the damned car?"

Roy Stevenson's outburst and the way he yanked at the knot of his tie betrayed his agitation. Adam kept studying the list of Visa card charges and didn't respond. He was even more restless and impatient than Roy—he just hid it better.

The need to find Jenna had been growing steadily since he realized that she'd taken the basset hound with her. Hope had fought a constant battle with wary pessimism for control of his emotions. As the hours wore on, hope had gained the upper hand. But only slightly. By the time she surfaced again, he'd probably be of no damned use to anybody, because he'd be confined to a padded cell.

They were waiting for Jenna to turn in the rented Plymouth. She hadn't used a credit card since Mount Vernon, Illinois. Or, if she had, the charge record hadn't yet been reported. She'd had the car for five days now. Every one of the rental agency's offices and drop-off locations had been alerted and provided with

Roy's office number; they would know within minutes after she turned in the Plymouth.

For now, all they could do was wait for the phone to ring and scan credit card reports. It was a lousy way to pass the time.

DENNIS BARNES'S JET landed at Evansville Regional Airport in southwestern Indiana at 7:16 p.m. Wednesday. A car and driver were waiting to take him the roughly sixty miles to Harrisburg, Illinois, where he checked into a motel as Bill Henderson, of Paducah, Kentucky. At precisely ten o'clock he answered two quick raps on the door and gestured Gordon Ross inside.

"Is she still there?" Barnes asked without any preliminaries, as he led the way to a round table in one corner.

"Yes, sir. She'd just gone back to the apartment when I left."

Barnes picked up a bottle of twelve-year-old bourbon and poured a shot into each of two plastic glasses. "A waitress," he said scornfully. He handed one of the glasses to Ross and indicated that he should sit. Ross hesitated a moment when he realized his employer intended to remain standing, then eased onto one of the flimsy wooden chairs. Barnes downed his bourbon in one swallow and poured another shot.

"She used to be my personal secretary, did you know that, Ross?"

Ross shook his head. "I don't know anything about her except what you told me—that I should keep tabs on her till you got here."

Barnes grunted softly in approval. "Her name's Kendra Jenner, but five years years ago the Justice Department moved her to St. Louis and gave her a new name—Jenna Kendrick. That was her reward for giving them what they needed to send me to prison."

Ross tossed back the bourbon in his glass. "Neither one of those is the name she's using now. She calls herself Susan Devers."

"Susan Devers." Barnes repeated the name with a slight smile of anticipation. "And you're sure she isn't on to you."

"Positive. I've been playing tourist, taking lots of pictures, disappearing for a couple hours every day, supposedly to go hiking. Only when I know she's at the restaurant, of course, which is most of the time. She's working a double shift until the woman who got burned comes back."

Barnes digested the information in silence and poured himself a third drink. "So as long as she doesn't know I've found her, she'll probably stay put," he speculated.

"Looks to me like she's settled in—for the time being, at least," Ross concurred. "She probably figures it's a good place to hide out." He eyed the bourbon bottle, shifted on the chair. "But I can't hang around much longer without drawing attention. This isn't the kind of place people come for a two-week vacation."

Barnes nodded. "Understood." His mouth curved in a humorless smile. "I gather it's also not the kind of place where kidnapping or murder would be a simple thing to carry off. This may take a few days to work out. It's possible the Feds have followed her. Not likely, but possible. They could even be using her as bait, hoping to draw me into the open. I'll send in a replacement if it looks like this will take more than another day or two to wrap up. Meanwhile, you go back to—what's the name of the place?''

"Utopia," Ross said dryly.

"Go back and keep watching her. There's no need to contact me so long as she sticks to her new routine. If she starts moving again, stay with her and report in when you get the chance. I plan to stay here for the next couple of days. If that changes, I'll get word to you."

Ross nodded, stood up and left. The meeting had taken less than ten minutes.

JESSE WAS DIVORCED. The marriage had lasted six and a half years. They hadn't had any kids. He'd wanted them; his wife hadn't. She was working for a big ad agency in Chicago now, making a damn sight more than his deputy sheriff's salary. He didn't begrudge her the money, but he was still ticked off about the fact that she'd cleaned out their joint checking account before she took off for the big city. His time would come, though; he was on the waiting list to take the state police exams. They'd probably work their way down to his name early next year.

Jesse managed to tell Jenna these things and more Wednesday night, feeding her dibs and dabs whenever she got two minutes' breathing space. He didn't realize it, but he told her a lot about himself, too, what kind of man he was. A picture was emerging, and it wasn't flattering.

"I'd've already been accepted by the state police," he confided, "but everybody knows they prefer not to take divorced men.'' Implying that his career disappointments were his ex-wife's fault, not his.

Jenna held her tongue and tried to strike a balance between appearing sympathetic and indifferent. No way was she going to encourage him, but she was afraid to freeze him out entirely. He was the type who would find a way to get back at her for bruising his masculine ego. All he had to do was make a note of the license plate number of her rented car, and then it would be only a hop, skip and jump to asking the St. Louis police to check for outstanding warrants or traffic tickets. It was doubtful that anyone would connect Susan Devers to Kendra-Jenna, but she couldn't afford to take any chances.

She had to play it cool and hope that eventually he would give up or get bored and find someone else to lavish his attention on. She would give it another couple of days before she decided to cut her losses and hit the road.

Thursday morning she got up early and met Tillie at the café to finalize the purchase of the Monarch. She would have to take the rented Plymouth to Marion, where, according to Eb, the nearest agency office was located. The trouble was, Marion was more than forty miles away.

''Do you think your son would be willing to follow me in the Mercury and bring me back here?''

Jenna was sitting with her back to the door, her attention on the other waitress, so she was surprised when a third voice joined the conversation—a by-now-familiar male voice.

''Follow you where?''

Jesse Herron slid onto the empty chair between the women, brightening their morning with one of his smiles as he placed his hat on the checkered table-cloth. He was out of uniform this morning, dressed in form-fitting indigo Levi's and a light blue plaid Western shirt. Apparently he hadn't been willing to leave the Stetson behind, though. Jenna wondered if he wore it to bed at night.

"Marion," Tillie answered before Jenna could silence her with a kick. "She just bought my Merc and now she has to turn in her rented car." To Jenna, she said, "Sorry, hon, but Davey's in school till three, and you'll be workin' then."

Jesse collected his hat and stood up. "Let's go."

Jenna stared at him helplessly. "Oh, but I couldn't impose—"

"No trouble at all," he assured her with an aw-shucks grin. "It's my day off, and I don't have anything better to do this morning. My truck's right outside."

Eb spoke up from the cash register, where he was counting money. "You'd better get moving, if you want to be back for the lunch crowd."

Jenna managed a feeble smile as she stood. "All right. I really appreciate this, Jesse."

His suggestive smile made her extremely nervous, as did his reply. "Always glad to help a pretty lady. Besides, the drive back will give us a chance to get to know each other better."

DENNIS BARNES GUIDED the powerful black touring sedan east on State Road 13, toward Muddy. Preoccupied with the news he'd received just before he left the motel, he took no notice of the traffic he passed headed the other way, including a white Plymouth driven by a woman with short, reddish hair.

The "travel writer" Kendra had become involved with back in St. Louis was none other than Adam Case, the man who'd headed the Justice Department's investigation five years ago. Obviously he'd gone to St. Louis to watch her, get close to her, but why? To provide protection? Not likely; the Marshals Service was already charged with that responsibility.

Adam Case's objectives weren't important, Barnes decided. What mattered was whether Case knew where she was. He hoped so. It would be an amazing stroke of luck to have the Organized Crime and Racketeering Section's chief investigator turn up in this Illinois backwater.

"Two birds with one stone," Barnes murmured with a cold smile. Yes, it would be an incredible stroke of luck.

"SO HOW DID SUCH a classy, obviously intelligent woman end up working as a waitress at Eb's Café in Utopia, Illinois?"

Jenna stared through the windshield and concentrated on keeping her body and her voice as relaxed as possible. She'd been expecting the question, sans the fawning flattery, since they left the café. She'd had the drive to Marion to prepare and was ready with an answer she hoped would satisfy his curiosity. It should. It was a true story.

"I'm on the run," she said quietly, and observed his surprised twitch from the corner of her eye.

"On the run? What'd you do, rob a bank?"

"Nothing so dramatic. I just had the bad judgment to marry a cruel, sadistic son of a bitch."

"Ahh, so it's your husband you're running from."

She nodded. "I packed a suitcase and left while he was out of town on business. It was the only option I had left. He refused to consider a divorce, threatened to kill me if he found out I'd even talked to an attorney. And he would have found out."

She paused for a moment when her voice developed a quaver. Maybe adapting the truth hadn't been such a terrific idea, after all. For three years she'd been a helpless spectator to Kayla's hellish life with Dennis Barnes, and now the frustrated rage she'd experienced then was welling up, threatening to overwhelm her.

"You think he really would've killed you?" Jesse asked. He sounded skeptical.

"I know it," Jenna said bitterly. "It would have been too great a blow to his ego to have the people he does business with know he couldn't hold on to his wife."

Jesse was silent for a minute or so. "Did he ever hit you?"

"Only once, to convince me his threats were serious. He takes a lot of pride in his self-control, and he was too smart to give me any bruises or broken bones."

"Sounds like you're the smart one, to get away from him like you did. You think he'll try to find you?"

"He would, if he had any idea where to look. I was careful to cover my tracks." She hesitated, wanting him to think she'd decided to confide in him because she felt she could trust him. "I changed my appearance, and I'm using a phony name."

Jesse glanced in surprise across the pickup's cab. "Susan Devers isn't your real name?"

She shook her head. "Don't ask me what it is, though. If I told you, you might accidentally use it sometime."

"But what about your job—you had to give Eb your Social Security number, didn't you?"

"Yes. But they hardly ever check to make sure the number and name match up. At least, that's what a tax accountant friend told me. Everything's computerized nowadays—we're nothing but a number to the government."

"That's for sure," he muttered. "And it isn't just the government. Bank account numbers, driver's license numbers, credit card numbers. You don't exist unless you can furnish the right number on demand."

"Right," Jenna said. "And so long as Eb uses my correct Social Security number, the taxes will be credited to me. I doubt if anybody will ever even notice that the name is different."

"Probably not," Jesse murmured cynically. "'Course, by the time we're ready to retire, there won't be any money left, anyway."

"You won't tell anybody, will you?" she asked anxiously, as if she'd had second thoughts about entrusting him with her secrets. "I haven't done anything really terrible, and the fewer people who know I'm hiding from my husband, the safer I'll be."

The gamble paid off. He let go of the steering wheel to reach across the seat and pat her knee. "Don't you worry," he assured her, suddenly transformed into the archetypal protective male. "I won't say a word. To anybody. And if the son of a gun does manage to track you down, he'll have to deal with me."

Jenna breathed a sigh of relief, and then another when his hand returned to the steering wheel.

"GOT HER!"

The exuberant shout came from Marv Bolander, who'd been covering the phones while Adam and Roy examined an enlarged road map spread out on the floor of Roy's office. They both looked up as Marv slammed the receiver on its cradle.

He waved a square of paper with a half-dozen words scribbled on it. "She just turned in the car at Marion, Illinois."

Adam hunkered over the map. "Where's Marion? How far?"

"There!" Roy's index finger almost jabbed a hole in the paper. "Looks like at least a hundred miles, maybe one-twenty."

"I-64 to I-57," Adam muttered under his breath. And then he was on his feet, grabbing the slip of paper from Marv as he headed for the door.

Roy scrambled up. "Wait! I can have a plane fueled and ready to go—"

Adam stopped long enough to make a terse response. "By the time I got to the airport, we filed a flight plan, waited in line to take off—" he gestured impatiently "—I could be halfway there. I'll check in from the rental-agency office."

"If you don't kill yourself on the way," Roy said as Adam strode across the outer office.

He drove like a maniac and made the 117-mile trip in just under an hour and a half. Of course, by the time he reached Marion, Jenna was long gone, but he got a detailed physical description of her from the young clerk behind the desk, as well as a description of the pickup truck she'd left in. The clerk thought he'd recognized the man driving the truck as a deputy sheriff from neighboring Saline County. Adam called Roy and passed on the information.

"Cut her hair, huh?" Roy said. He sounded unexpectedly chipper. "Now, that's a shame, though I'm sure she looks terrific as a redhead. Hang on a sec, I want to check the map." Adam waited with barely contained impatience for several seconds. When Roy came back on the line, he muttered enigmatically, "Yep, Saline County checks. Listen, since you're already in southern Illinois, how would you feel about making a little trip over to Utopia?"

Adam snapped to attention, his impatience forgotten. "What's in Utopia?"

"Not what—who. Susan Devers. At least, she was there a couple of days ago—used a charge card to buy gas."

Adam begged a pen and paper from the clerk behind the desk and wrote down the particulars, then hung up and asked for directions. He was back on the road in less than two minutes. Only then did he start to worry about how Jenna would react when he approached her. His imagination furnished all sorts of possibilities, from screamed curses to frigid silence to headlong flight. Reminding himself that she'd taken the basset hound, he goosed the Mustang up to sixty, which was as fast as he calculated he could safely navigate the two-lane asphalt highway.

BARNES AND GORDON ROSS watched from the laundromat across the street as Jenna alighted from the pickup truck and entered Eb's Café. Ross had brought two loads of dirty laundry as cover. The man driving the truck continued on down the street.

"The deputy?" Barnes asked.

"Yeah. According to the waitress I told you about, the one named Louise, he's been comin' on to her, but so far she's given him the cold shoulder. Louise is convinced she's crazy," he added with a sneer. "Seems most of the ladies think Deputy Herron would be quite a catch."

"He must be thirty-five. How come he's still single?"

"His wife divorced him three or four years ago. Took everything but the fillings in his teeth first, though. Closed their joint bank account and had her brothers load most of their furniture into a van while he was on patrol. He came home, opened the door— 'Hi, honey, what's for dinner?'—and got the surprise of his life. But the worst part is—you'll love this—he runs back out to his patrol car and calls it in as a robbery." Ross paused, shook his head. "He's a jerk with a Wyatt Earp complex, but still, you have to feel sorry for the poor sap. He must have felt like the world's biggest fool."

Barnes was silent for several minutes after the narrative ended. He stared at the diner across the street, his eyes narrowed and a contemplative frown drawing his brows together. When Ross had first told him about the deputy who'd been sniffing around Kendra, he'd been concerned that the man would be a problem, an unwelcome complication. But now... He just might be able to use Deputy Herron.

"Find out where he lives," Barnes instructed. "And keep pumping this Louise for information. See if she knows what they talked about during their little trip today."

"Sure," Ross replied. "But I can only talk to her in the mornings, before Susan—er, that is, Kendra—starts work. It was a lucky accident that she came in this morning and I heard them talking about returning the rental car."

Barnes flicked a manicured hand impatiently. "Get as much information as you can in the next twenty-four hours and then leave, before somebody starts to get suspicious."

"What about you?" Ross asked anxiously. "Surely you don't intend to stay in town?"

"Not tonight. Tomorrow I may take over your room. I have a feeling the Feds will show up before long. It might take them another day, maybe two. I'll have to finish my business and be gone before they arrive." He turned from the window and fixed Ross with a glacial stare. "Finish your laundry and then find out where Deputy Dog lives. I'm going back to the motel. Report to me there."

Chapter Eleven

Friday morning Jenna sat at the small table at the kitchen end of her living room to take stock of her capital. She still had several hundred in cash in addition to the certified checks, which were now stashed in Adam, Jr.'s tummy. It wasn't as secure a hiding place as the document safe she'd left in St. Louis, but the apartment was far from burglarproof, and she hadn't wanted to carry the checks around with her.

She made a mental note to exchange some of the larger bills for smaller denominations before she left the café tonight. Since she'd stopped moving she had been trying to pay for everything with cash, but she'd had to use a credit card on Tuesday because the gas station attendant didn't have change for a fifty. Now she made sure to keep a supply of ones, fives and tens in her wallet.

It was time to walk to the café for her first shift. She moved the basset hound to the sofa, gave him a good-bye pat on the nose, collected her purse and left.

ADAM HAD WATCHED from the shadows under a giant maple tree across the street when she returned from work the night before. She'd looked dead on her feet. For a few seconds he'd had to forcibly restrain himself from dashing across the pavement, sweeping her up in his arms and carrying her into the shabby, cramped apartment that was serving as her home. The main reason he'd stayed put was because he suspected she'd start yelling bloody murder the instant she spotted him.

The apartment had probably started out as a small garage, or maybe a tool shed. It sat at the end of a gravel drive on the back of the lot, behind a neat frame house. The house was unoccupied. He wondered why she hadn't rented it instead, until he peeked in one of the dusty rear windows and saw that there was no furniture. Adam wasn't happy with the apartment's location or its utter lack of security. The locks were a joke, there was no outside light, and a hundred-pound weakling would be able to lift out the window air conditioner and climb inside in less than a minute.

Friday morning, he was standing at the window of his cabin at the motor inn, a pair of high-powered binoculars covering the top half of his face, when she left for the short walk to the café. She exchanged nods of greeting with a tall, sunburned blond man who was leaving as she arrived. There was something familiar about the man....

Adam kept the binoculars trained on him as he strolled down the main street, apparently headed for the motor inn. When the man reached the drive, Adam stepped back from the window, but kept watching. He was positive he knew this guy from somewhere. And then suddenly he remembered. He was one of Dennis Barnes's lackeys.... Ross, that was his name. George, Greg—Gordon! Gordon Ross. Adam had never come face-to-face with him during the investigation, but he'd seen Ross's photo often enough to recognize him now.

He lowered the binoculars, edging to one side of the window as Ross walked straight to the cabin next door and let himself in with a key. The drapes were drawn, making it impossible to see inside. Was he alone? Each cabin had a gravel drive that ran along the north side. Adam had pulled his Mustang all the way back, so that it wouldn't be visible from the street. By craning his neck, he could see the back end of a Jeep with Illinois plates parked beside the cabin next door.

Jenna was safely inside the café, and would be there for some time. He decided to hike down to the dry-goods store and do a little shopping. He hadn't stopped on the way out of St. Louis to pack a bag. As he passed the cabin next to his, he glanced around casually, checking to see if there was another vehicle parked in front of the Jeep. There wasn't. If Barnes was in town, he must be staying someplace else.

DENNIS BARNES HAD LEFT the motor inn before six-thirty to be sure he caught Jesse Herron before he left for work. The deputy was buttoning his uniform shirt when he answered the door with a respectful "Something I can do for you, sir?"

"As a matter of fact, there is," Barnes replied. "We've never met, but I believe you know my wife. She's working at one of the restaurants in town, using the name Susan Devers."

Jesse stiffened, his amiable expression instantly downshifting to a frown. Barnes hastily held up a hand.

"I'd be willing to bet she's told you some pretty terrible things about me, most if not all of which are barefaced lies. I'd like you to give me fifteen minutes of your time. After you've heard what I have to say, if you tell me to get lost, I'll go."

The deputy pursed his lips, clearly taken aback and unsure how to respond.

"Please, hear me out, that's all I'm asking. There are two sides to every story. Listen to mine, then make up your own mind which one to believe. Just give me fifteen minutes. As a favor, one man to another."

Twelve minutes later, Jesse sat on one end of his cheap, plaid-upholstered sofa, gazing at the photo of a young boy Barnes had removed from his wallet.

"It's hard to believe she's done the things you say," he muttered.

Barnes heaved a defeated sigh. "You don't believe me." He reached over and took the photo from Jesse's hand. "I can't say I'm surprised. A beautiful woman can convince a man of just about anything, especially if she happens to have the face of an angel."

Jesse frowned. "No. I mean, I do believe you. It's just . . . like you said, she's very convincing. She told me you'd threatened to kill her."

Barnes laughed bitterly. "That's rich. She cleans out my safe, abandons our son, and *I* end up being the villain."

"I thought it was strange that she had so much money," Jesse said. "She paid cash for both the car she bought and the one she rented, and she gave Eb a month's deposit *and* the first month's rent for the apartment. Thirty thousand dollars! Whew! I sympathize with you, Bill, I really do. My ex—''

Barnes cut him off before he could stray from the subject at hand. ''I can't let her get away with it, Jesse. I've put up with her compulsive lying and the other men, taken her back after she disappeared for days at a time. But this was the last straw.'' He glanced down at the photo of Thad. ''Bill, Jr.'s the only reason I'm reluctant to press charges. She'll never be the world's greatest mother, but she's the only one he's got.''

''He'd be better off with no mother,'' Jesse commented.

''Maybe so,'' Barnes said with a sigh. ''My mind's ninety percent made-up. But before I talk to a lawyer, I have to see her one more time, face-to-face, give her a chance to return whatever's left of the thirty thousand.'' He paused, fixed the deputy with a level look. ''Will you help me?''

''It would be my pleasure,'' Jesse said grimly.

''Great!'' Barnes grabbed the other man's hand and shook it vigorously, then opened his wallet. ''I want to give you a little something to show my appreciation.''

''Oh, no.'' Jesse shook his head in denial, but stopped when he saw the currency stuffed into the wallet. ''Really,'' he said with a shade less enthusiasm. ''That's not necessary.''

Barnes withdrew three one-hundred-dollar bills and pressed them into the other man's hand. ''I insist. If you won't take it as a gift, think of it as a commission, a sort of tax-free finder's fee.''

Deputy Herron mumbled a weak protest, but he didn't return the money. They worked out a few details, and then Barnes returned to the motor inn. He parked in a deserted alleyway behind the office and was back in the cabin when Ross finished his early lunch, paid the bill and left Eb's Café.

"I THOUGHT WE COULD go rock-climbing Sunday. I've got the afternoon off, and Eb tells me Nora should be back at work by then."

Jenna didn't reply until she'd placed Jesse's plate lunch in front of him. This was it, the crunch she'd known would come sooner or later.

"I don't think so, Jesse," she murmured. "Not that the invitation isn't flattering. You're a terrific guy, but I'm not ready to start seeing anybody just yet."

He gave her one of his knock-'em-dead smiles. "Hey, did I say it was a date? I won't put any moves on you—promise. Just think of it as spending an afternoon with a friend. Sunshine, fresh air, the great outdoors. You've been cooped up in here all week. It'd do you good to get out."

She shook her head with an apologetic smile. "Thanks, really, but I don't think so."

His tenacious insistence troubled Jenna. She sensed that if she hadn't moved away to wait on another table, he'd have kept pushing until she either said yes or was forced to be rude. She wasn't surprised, really, just depressed and disappointed. She'd known from the day they met that Jesse Herron's pride wouldn't tolerate the slightest hint of rejection. She suspected he would try again when he came in for dinner and keep after her until she gave him the answer he wanted. If she continued to turn him down, he might try to find her fictitious husband, just to get even. Or worse, report her to the Social Security Administration. What was the penalty, she wondered, for impersonating someone who'd been dead more than twenty-five years?

She was going to have to leave Utopia, Illinois, sooner than she'd expected.

By four-thirty she had a tension headache that made her both snappish and clumsy. When she dropped a tray of forks and promptly fired off a string of curses, Eb told her to go home and lie down for an hour. Jenna went gladly.

She made a quick trip to the grocery store for bread, lunch meat, cheese, milk and a package of chocolate cookies before heading for her apartment. The milk and cookies were for later, when she got off work for the night and needed some serious comfort food. She was staring morosely at the ground, worrying about where she would go when she left town, so she didn't realize a car was parked in the driveway until she walked into the rear bumper.

She swore, rubbed her right kneecap…and then got a good look at the car and almost dropped the bag of groceries. It was a 1966 Mustang with the original Tahoe Turquoise paint. Shock ricocheted through her, followed quickly by a bolt of panic. There couldn't be two cars like that in the entire Midwest.

She glanced over her shoulder, toward the street. Should she turn around and run, before he saw her? Stupid idea. Where would she go? She still hadn't collected the keys to the Mercury, or the Mercury itself either, for that matter. Tillie's son was supposed to deliver it to her at the café tonight. He'd volunteered to wash and wax it for her. Nice of him, but at that moment she'd have given anything for a grungy, oil-burning pile of junk, so long as the engine ran and it had a full tank of gas.

This couldn't be happening. Adam, here! How had he found her? What did he want? Was he alone?

She wasn't going to get answers to those questions by standing out here in the driveway. But, God, she didn't want to go inside, have to look at him again, share that small space with him. The prospect made her stomach churn. Memories rose like wisps of fog. Jenna ruthlessly repressed them, took a deep, fortifying breath and stepped around the Mustang.

She heard the music as she unlocked the door—one of the Righteous Brothers albums that had come with the apartment. Adam was standing next to the couch, holding the basset hound. He lifted his head. Their eyes met. It was worse than she'd feared it would be. A storm of emotions raged inside her: joy; intense, burning anger; scalding pain. The pain became dominant as she took in his long, lean body, the beard stubble and his somber, watchful expression.

"I hope you got enough for two," he said, inclining his head to indicate the brown paper bag she carried. His drawl affected her like salt on an open wound. "I'm starved."

Jenna believed him. He looked like he hadn't eaten or slept in days. She hardened her heart, reminding herself that he'd deliberately used and deceived her and had probably tracked her down so he could do more of the same.

"What the hell are you doing here?" she asked as she walked to the kitchen and set the bag next to the sink. After that first, devastating glance, she was careful not to look directly at him.

"Saving your life, more than likely."

"Don't do me any favors."

She could feel his eyes on her, and it made her want to scream, throw something, fly at him in a red-hot rage.... To keep herself from doing any of those things, she concentrated on putting the groceries away, while Bobby Hatfield wailed from the stereo about how his lover had made him leave his happy home. Welcome to the club, Bobby, she was tempted to say. Love stinks, doesn't it?

"I realize you'd prefer to let the local deputy deal with Barnes for you," Adam said coldly, "but I seriously doubt he's up to the job."

She whirled to face him at the reference to Jesse Herron, eyes flashing. Then the word *Barnes* sank in. The blood drained from her face.

"He's here?"

Adam took a couple of steps toward her before the warning in her eyes stopped him. "If he isn't, he soon will be."

"Damn you!" Jenna said in a low, furious voice. "You led him right to me, didn't you? Was that part of the plan all along?"

Adam scowled and set the basset hound on the dinette table. "He didn't need me to lead him to you. He's known every move you've made since you closed out Kendra Jenner's savings account last Saturday."

"I don't believe you! Why should I? Every word you've ever spoken to me has been a lie!"

Something flashed for an instant in Adam's eyes. If he'd been anyone else, she'd have thought it was regret. But hard-nosed Justice Department drones didn't feel regret. She suspected they were purged of that emotion, along with their compassion and integrity, during their indoctrination.

"Not quite every word," he said quietly. And then, before she could challenge the claim, he added, "Barnes has had you watched for years, maybe since you moved to St. Louis. How do you think he knew about the Kendra Jenner account?"

"You probably told him."

"That's an idiotic thing to say! Why the hell would I—"

"The same reason you did everything else—so you could catch him doing something that would justify sending him back to prison. Why did you lie to me? Why did you use your oily charm to worm your way into my life, then monopolize every spare minute of my time? Did you read my mail, Adam? Did you tap my phone?"

His expression became more grim with each condemnation she hurled at him. "No," he said when she stopped for breath. "I didn't read your mail or tap your phone."

"Couldn't convince a judge to issue a court order?" Jenna asked sarcastically. She didn't wait for an answer—he'd probably lie, anyway. She dodged around him to go to the small closet next to the bathroom.

"What do you think you're doing?" he asked as she yanked clothes off hangers and tossed them onto the sofa.

"What does it look like I'm doing? I'll give you the benefit of the doubt and assume you didn't tell Barnes where I was. To be honest, I have trouble believing even you would sink that low. But you just said that if he isn't here already, he soon will be. I *would* be an idiot to wait around for him."

"So you're going to run again."

"You got it, Tex." She dragged the tan suitcase from the closet shelf and set it on the far end of the couch. "I'd decided to move on in a day or two, anyway. The deputy you mentioned is starting to make a nuisance of himself, and frankly, I've had my fill of smooth-talking John Law types."

She threw open the suitcase and began tossing in clothes. Adam suddenly moved, so fast that she jumped in reaction. He slammed down the lid of the suitcase.

"I hope you're prepared to spend the rest of your life running," he said in a hard, uncompromising tone. "Because you'll have to. Barnes won't give up. Ever. You know that. He's obsessed with revenge, and he has the resources to track you down no matter where you go. No matter how long it takes or how much it costs. He'll find you, Jenna. Sooner or later he'll find you, and when he does he'll kill you."

Adam watched her flinch as the words hammered home, watched her start to fall apart and then pull herself back together. He hated himself for assaulting her like this, on top of the hurt he'd already inflicted, but there was no time for calm, reasonable persuasion. The mood she was in, she would refuse to listen, anyway. Everything he'd said was the truth, and the cornered look in her wide, frightened eyes told him she knew it. He wanted more than anything to take her in his arms, but he knew she would fight him. So he stood tense and unmoving, waiting for some kind of response. She folded her arms tightly under her breasts and lifted her chin, telegraphing both defensiveness and defiance. Adam prayed for patience.

"And I suppose you have a master plan that will miraculously provide a happy ending for everybody, except, of course, Dennis Barnes. That's your specialty, isn't it—devising Machiavellian schemes to keep him in prison for the rest of his life? You're every bit as obsessive as he is."

"And you're no slouch when it comes to Machiavellian schemes," Adam returned. "Very few people would have the brains or the nerve to create a whole new identity for themselves. The entire plan was clever as hell, but the crowning touch was faking your own death. That was really ingenious."

"Thank you," Jenna said tightly. "Coming from you, I suppose that's quite a compliment."

He ignored her sarcasm. At least she was talking to him. "It probably would have worked, too, if Barnes hadn't known about the Kendra Jenner bank account. You should have transferred the money to an account in Susan's name as soon as you had the necessary ID."

"Unfortunately, it didn't occur to me," she said bitterly. "But you have to remember that I was operating at a disadvantage. I didn't have the benefit of your expert advice."

Adam absorbed the dig without any visible reaction. Let her get her shots in, he told himself. She's entitled. He knew he wouldn't have a chance of winning her back so long as she felt this bitter resentment. Maybe if she got it out of her system . . .

"So what's your plan?" she asked bluntly.

"I don't have one."

She expelled a harsh, humorless laugh. "Great. In that case, would you please move out of the way so I can finish packing?"

She opened the suitcase and picked up a pair of jeans. He impulsively reached out and clasped her arm, holding on when she would have pulled away.

"Jenna, please."

Jenna reluctantly lifted her gaze to his face, then had to summon every ounce of willpower she possessed to resist the appeal in his fathomless eyes. His fingers were like brands on her arm, his stubbled jaw mere inches from her mouth. Damn him, how could he still affect her like this? In spite of everything—the knowledge that he'd betrayed her, the incredible pain he'd caused her—she wanted nothing more at that moment than to feel his arms close around her.

"I can help you," he said softly. "I'm the only one who can help you. But you have to trust me."

She shook her head helplessly. Did he have any idea what he was asking?

"Please." It was a fervent whisper, almost a prayer. "Trust me."

"You lied to me," she accused, her voice thick with imminent tears.

"Yes."

"Used me. You thought I conspired with him!"

His fingers tightened on her arm. "Yes. That's what I thought, when I went to St. Louis. But if you'd stayed in Roy's office a few minutes longer, you'd have heard me tell him I knew I'd been wrong."

She closed her eyes, partly to stem the tears and partly to shut out his tense, earnest expression. If she believed him, and he was lying again...

"No." She tried to tug her arm free, but he refused to let her go. "I can't trust you. I *won't* trust you! You just want to use me again. You're obsessed with catching Dennis Barnes, and you don't care who you hurt in the process."

Without warning he grabbed her other arm and shook her, hard. Her eyes flew open as she gasped.

"Damn you!" he swore through clenched teeth. "You think you're the only one who's been hurting? You let me believe you were *dead!* What do you think this past week's been like for me?"

Hell. He didn't have to say it, it was written on his face—the bloodshot eyes and bruised half-moons beneath them, the hollows under his high, slanting cheeks, the dark growth of beard....

"You have to trust me, dammit!" he snarled into her face. "You don't have any choice! He knows you're here. If you run, he'll be right behind you."

Jenna was too stunned to speak for several moments. What had happened to the easygoing, good-humored Texan who'd spent a week and a half charming her socks off, wooed her with a monstrous bouquet and a stuffed dog, taken her roller-skating and to the zoo? The Adam Case confronting her now was another animal altogether—passionate, tempestuous, a force to be reckoned with. She knew without a shred of doubt that she could trust him with her life. The question was, could she trust him with her heart?

"So help me," she said, the slightest hint of a tremor in her voice, "if you hurt me again—"

He pulled her against him so hard and so fast that her head flew back and the rest of the warning was lost, along with her breath. For long seconds he just held her, so tightly that she could feel the buttons of his shirt and the heavy thud of his heart. Jenna closed her eyes and wrapped her arms around his waist.

"Never," he muttered into her hair. He kissed the top of her head, more than once, then loosened his crushing embrace just enough to gain access to her mouth.

"Never," he repeated as his lips closed over hers. He kissed her long and deep and hard, draining her and replenishing her, erasing the last vestige of her uncertainty and replacing it with soaring exultation. When he finally eased his mouth from hers, Jenna clung to him to keep from falling.

"I love you," he said in a raspy murmur. "If you'd stayed around, you'd have heard me tell Roy that, too."

She gave him a watery smile. "You told Uncle Roy you love him?"

His grin was a flash of the old Adam, but then he saw the moisture leaking from her eyes. "Oh, baby, don't. Please." He kissed her eyelids, her cheeks, remorse in his voice and the tender caress of his lips. "God, I'm sorry. You'll never know. Please don't cry."

Jenna's breath caught on a little sob of joy, which seemed to increase his distress. She wanted to tell him it was all right, that *she* was all right, that those three priceless syllables had healed her bruised heart and filled the dark, empty places inside her with light. But at the moment, words were awkward, inadequate tools. She impulsively grabbed his head and gave him a deep, lingering kiss instead.

"It's okay," she said against his lips. "They're good tears."

He pulled back to look into her eyes. "Good tears?"

"Yeah." She gave him a beatific smile, which apparently convinced him. He kissed her again and neither of them was inclined to speak for quite some time. But when their breathing quickened and soft moans replaced blissful sighs, Jenna leaned back against his arms.

"I have to be back at work in—" she glanced over his shoulder at her watch "—half an hour."

Adam released her with a reluctant sigh. "Then we'd better grab a couple of sandwiches and put our heads together. We need to come up with a plan, and fast."

"I have absolute confidence in you, Tex," she assured him.

Chapter Twelve

She was singing a different tune fifteen minutes later.

"You call that a plan? Using me as *bait?*"

Over bologna-and-cheese sandwiches he'd told her about Gordon Ross—that Ross had been watching her since she arrived in Utopia and might have followed her all the way from St. Louis—and that he was convinced Ross's presence meant Barnes himself would shortly be making an appearance.

In turn, she had told him about Jesse Herron. Adam thought their best bet would be to enlist the deputy's help in luring Barnes into the open.

"Wouldn't that be entrapment?" Jenna had asked suspiciously.

"No, for a couple of reasons. First, as soon as Barnes shows his face outside Maryland, he's violated the terms of his parole, which would be enough to send him back to jail. And second, Herron wouldn't be enticing him to do something he isn't already planning. Jesse Herron's a cop," he reasoned. "Sworn to uphold the law. And from what you've told me about him, I expect he'll jump at the chance to help bring in a federal fugitive."

Jenna frowned as she bit into a cookie. "But why do we have to do this in the middle of a national wilderness area? Why can't you just stay here and wait for Barnes to come after me?"

"Because he won't," Adam said flatly. "Especially after the close call he had back in St. Louis. If something happened to you in a small town like this—something violent—everybody would know about it immediately. The state and county police would set up roadblocks and seal off the entire area. The locals might even grab their hunting rifles and shotguns and join the manhunt." He shook his head firmly.

"Barnes doesn't mind taking calculated risks, but the odds would be stacked too heavily against him. This isn't St. Louis. He couldn't just lay low for a couple of days and wait for the excitement to blow over."

Everything he said made sense, but Jenna still wasn't thrilled with his so-called plan. "I don't like it, Adam. Too much could go wrong. Neither of us knows the area. What if you got lost, or lost Jesse and me, and Barnes got to us first? What if he brings this Ross guy along?"

He shook his head again. "Ross checked out of the motor inn and left town this afternoon."

"Which guarantees he won't come back?" she asked cynically. "I know Dennis Barnes, remember, maybe better than you do. He'll think of every possibility. Whatever you come up with, he'll have already anticipated and prepared for."

Adam raked a hand through his hair in exasperation. "No plan is perfect, Jenna, but Barnes isn't superhuman."

"No, he's merely a brilliant psychopath who keeps managing to slip away from the government agents assigned to watch him," she snapped. "And this plan had better be as close to perfect as we can make it, or you can count me out. In case it's slipped your mind, *I'm* the one Dennis Barnes wants to murder."

His fist slammed down on the table, almost overturning her glass of milk. "Dammit!" he exploded. "If I could think of anything else that had a chance in hell of working, we'd do it!"

The outburst brought Jenna's stubborn resistance to a screeching halt. "All right," she murmured. "Take it easy. Maybe I'm not giving—"

But he wasn't in the mood to be placated. "If you've got a better idea, I'd love to hear it. I'd rather go up against Barnes and his entire army of goons alone and unarmed than put you at risk. Unfortunately, that isn't an option. If we don't draw him into the open now, while we've got the chance, he'll just bide his time until you move on, or leave town to do some shopping or go to a movie or have dinner in a nice restaurant. Dammit, Jenna," he said in frustration, "this is the best I can come up with."

She looked into his haggard face and wondered what she had done to deserve such a man. She also asked herself what was more frightening—the dangerous scheme he was proposing, or the prospect of looking over her shoulder for the rest of her life?

"All right," she said softly. She laid her hand over his clenched fist. "We'll do it."

ADAM LOCATED Deputy Herron's house just before dusk and drove past, thinking he would have to come back later. The deputy already had company; there was a dark, late-model car parked in front of the house, next to the pickup truck Jesse had been driving yesterday.

He turned around at the next driveway he came to and headed back to town. But as he passed by the second time, he glanced to the right and abruptly slowed the Mustang. The dusk-to-dawn light in Jesse's front yard had just come on, clearly illuminating the Missouri license plate on the car. Maybe it was only coincidence that Jesse had a visitor from St. Louis County. And maybe not.

Adam recalled what Mrs. Thompson from across the street had told the police officers the night Barnes came to Jenna's house. *"All I can tell you about the car is that it was dark—black or midnight blue. Dark and big, a Buick or an Oldsmobile, I think. One of the expensive models."*

The car parked in front of Jesse Herron's house was a black Olds touring sedan.

He drove a couple of hundred feet before he found a gap in the trees crowding the road that was wide enough to pull the Mustang into, then got out and circled around to approach the house from the rear. Luckily, Deputy Herron didn't appear to have a dog. Adam sprinted across fifty feet of overgrown back yard and cautiously made his way along the north side of the house, toward the one window that showed light.

The thought crossed his mind that if Jesse heard him sneaking around out here, the deputy might understandably take him for a prowler and decide to get in some target practice. He was careful to test the ground before committing his weight on each step, and hoped Jesse hadn't left a garden hose or hoe lying around. He reached the lighted window without tripping over anything and discovered that his luck was holding; the bottom sash was raised several inches, allowing him to eavesdrop on the conversation taking place inside.

"You have to try again. I know you can do it, Jesse."

Adam's forehead furrowed in concentration. The voice was familiar, but he couldn't immediately place it.

"I don't know, Bill." The second man—Jesse Herron, he presumed—sounded less than enthusiastic. "She was pretty definite. Gave me a song and dance about how she isn't ready to start seeing anybody just yet. You know, because of her abusive husband."

Adam moved a few inches away from the wall, trying to get a look at the man Jesse was speaking to.

"She's pulling your chain, Jesse, making you work for it, that's all. It's a game with her. If you give up too easily, she figures you weren't serious in the first place."

"You mean she's just playing hard to get?" Jesse replied. He didn't sound convinced.

Adam couldn't make any sense of the conversation. What was going on here? They were obviously talking about Jenna. She'd told him about Jesse's invitation to go rock-climbing and her refusal. That was what gave him the idea to enlist the deputy's help.

"Exactly! She wants to keep you off balance, never sure where you stand with her."

"Well, it's working," Jesse muttered.

The men were sitting at a right angle to one another. Adam had a clear view of the side of the deputy's face and the back of the other man's head. He had dark, slightly wavy hair. Adam wished the guy would move or, better yet, get up and walk around. He told himself it couldn't be Dennis Barnes. A second later the man shifted, leaning forward and to the right, and he was proved wrong.

"I can see you're discouraged," Barnes said. He glanced down, toward his lap. "What you need is a little more motivation."

"No, Bill." The deputy's uneasy protest made Adam tense in apprehension. Had Barnes pulled a gun on him?

"No, no, I insist," Barnes said firmly. "I'm a businessman, Jesse. I consider this an investment. Would another five hundred be enough to motivate you, you think?" Jesse didn't reply, but Adam saw the covetous expression that tautened his handsome features.

"Tell you what," Barnes continued with the smooth confidence of a street hustler. "How about five hundred now and another five hundred when you bring her to me?"

Adam felt like he'd been punched in the gut. He held his breath as he waited for the deputy's reaction. Jesse stared at whatever Barnes was holding—evidently a wad of cash—and licked his lips. Adam's hands clenched into fists when he saw the unconscious gesture. Don't do it! he wanted to shout. You're a cop, for God's sake!

But he remained silent when Jesse reached out and took what Barnes was offering. He felt sick with anger and disgust.

"I knew I could count on you, Jesse," Barnes murmured. "Now I think we should try to work out a few details. I'll need some kind of map, so I'll know where to meet you."

ADAM'S CAR WAS NOWHERE in sight when Jenna parked in the driveway a few minutes after ten, and there were no lights showing from inside the apartment. She tried to quell her disappointment as she let herself in.

He was sitting on the couch, in the dark. When she turned on the overhead light and saw him, she almost jumped out of her skin. Then she took in his solemn expression.

"What's wrong?" she asked, dropping her purse on an end table and sinking down beside him.

"Did you tell Jesse you'd go rock-climbing on Sunday?"

"Yes," Jenna murmured. The fact that he hadn't yet taken her in his arms, or even kissed her hello, worried her as much as the grim set of his mouth. "That was the plan, wasn't it?"

Adam grimaced. "The plan didn't take into account the possibility that Jesse might already be working for Barnes."

"If that's supposed to be a joke—" she began.

"It's no joke." He told her what he'd seen and heard at Jesse Herron's house.

Jenna stared at him helplessly. "What are we going to do?"

Adam sighed and slid his arm around her shoulders, pulling her against him. "For the time being, there's not much we can do. I tried to follow Barnes

when he left Jesse's. But by the time I got back to
where I'd hidden my car, he was long gone. I looked
for the Olds when I got back to town. There's no sign
of it. He's probably put a safe distance between himself and Jesse Herron, in case Jesse gets cold feet between now and Sunday afternoon.''

"You think there's a chance he might?" she asked
hopefully.

"I think we can stack the odds in our favor by setting him straight about Dennis Barnes. Barnes lied to
him, claimed to be your husband, Bill Something-or-
other, and fed Jesse a story about your having run out
on him—after you'd taken a truckload of his money.''

"Great," Jenna muttered. "He must have found
out Jesse's ex-wife did exactly that. He would know
just which buttons to push," she said bitterly. "And
the story *I* told Jesse probably made him more inclined to believe Barnes.''

Adam gave her a comforting hug. "But if I can get
Jesse alone for ten minutes and set him straight, we
may still have a shot at convincing him to help us. The
trouble is, he's disappeared. By the time I gave up
trying to find Barnes, he'd left the café. I went back to
the motor inn and tried to call him, but either he isn't
answering the phone or he's not home. I figured I'd
wait for you to get off work, then the two of us could
drive out to his place.''

"It would be a waste of time," Jenna said.
"Louise—she's the morning waitress—hooked up
with him at the café and they left together.''

"Do you have any idea where they went?"

She shook her head. "Louise let me know she intended to make it a hot date, though. I think she sees

me as the competition," she added dryly. "Apparently she's had her eye on Jesse Herron since his divorce. Judging by the gleam in her eye, I'd say he'll be lucky to make it home before sunup."

Adam fell into a meditative silence that lasted several minutes, his hand absently stroking her arm as he considered what to do next. Jenna rested her head on his shoulder, but she didn't distract him with questions or suggestions. She was worried—she'd have been a fool not to be—but oddly enough, the knowledge that Barnes had managed to trick Jesse Herron into helping him didn't throw her into a panic. She wasn't alone anymore, with only her wits and blind instinct to protect her. Adam was with her now. Whatever happened, they would face it together. Just knowing that brought her a peace she hadn't felt in five long years.

"Jenna," he whispered. "Are you asleep?"

She lifted her head and kissed his bristly jaw. "No," she said huskily. "Just thinking about how lucky I am."

His right eyebrow rose a quizzical centimeter. "Lucky?"

"Mmm-hmm." She wrapped her arms around his waist. "I'd even go so far as to say blessed. I love you, Adam Case."

The arm around her shoulders tightened spasmodically. He closed his eyes and rested his forehead against hers for a moment. "I love you, too. That's why I'm having second thoughts about this half-baked plan."

"I'm not," she said, softly but with utter conviction.

"Jenna."

Sensing that he was about to catalog all the reasons the scheme wouldn't work, she pressed her fingers across his lips. "No, don't. We've covered all that already. I want this over with, Adam. I want to be free to get on with my life, to know I can do what I want, go where I want, without having to worry that Dennis Barnes might be waiting around every corner. He's already taken five years of my life. That's enough. I'm not willing to give him any more."

He kissed her fingers, then clasped her hand and pulled it away. "I understand. But if something goes wrong on Sunday—hell, if *anything* goes wrong—you could be killed."

"We both could be," she countered. "So we'd better make damned sure nothing goes wrong."

He continued to hold her hand, stroking her palm with the pad of his thumb as he looked deep into her eyes. For a while she thought he would argue, try to convince her to get away now, while she could, maybe go back to St. Louis. But finally his mouth relaxed, then quirked in a small, slanting smile.

"Have you always been so hardheaded?" he drawled.

"Only about things that really matter. So, what's our next move?"

"I think I'd better give old Uncle Roy a call. And since you don't have a telephone, I'll have to do it from the motor inn."

"While you're there, why don't you check out?" she suggested impulsively. "You could stay here until Sunday."

"Why, Miz Kendrick, are you suggestin' we shack up together?" he teased. "Live in *sin?*"

Jenna ducked her head to hide her smile. "Actually," she murmured demurely, "what I meant was that I'd feel a lot safer having you under the same roof." She paused a beat, lifted her head just enough to give him a seductive look from beneath lowered lashes. "But now that you mention it, the sin part does sound ... interesting."

Adam laughed and dragged her into his arms for a kiss that left her flushed and breathless. "Doesn't it, though?" he said in the sexiest voice she'd ever heard. Abruptly releasing her, he stood up. "I'll be happy to accept your indecent proposal, ma'am, but I have to keep the cabin, for the phone. Think lascivious thoughts while I'm gone."

Jenna pulled the basset hound onto her lap as the door closed behind him. "It's going to be all right, Junior," she said, nuzzling the toy's plush fur. "We'll *make* it all right."

BILL HENDERSON, of Paducah, Kentucky, was back in his Harrisburg motel room when Jesse Herron called from a pay phone outside Eb's Café to give him the news that his wife had changed her mind and agreed to go rock-climbing on Sunday.

Jesse had sounded extremely pleased with himself, which worried Dennis Barnes. The last thing he needed was for the deputy to get too cocky and spook her into running again. He advised Jesse to make himself scarce until it was time to pick her up Sunday afternoon, in case she changed her mind again. At first Jesse balked, but in the course of boasting about how he'd enticed "Susan" to reconsider his invitation, he mentioned that he'd had to be not only charming as hell, but also tactful, because one of the other waitresses had come into the café and started flirting with him in the middle of his pitch.

It wasn't difficult to convince Jesse that taking the other woman out would help cement Susan's commitment for Sunday. "Competition always brings out her aggressiveness," Barnes had assured the deputy. "Make sure she sees you coming on to this Louise and then leaving with her."

Jesse readily accepted the advice, then confided that Louise *was* a good-looking woman, so it wouldn't be any great hardship to show her a good time.

When Barnes hung up, he reflected contemptuously that it was a wonder crime wasn't rampant in southeastern Illinois, considering the intelligence level of the local law-enforcement personnel.

Shortly before eleven o'clock, he answered a knock at the door and admitted a messenger from Nolan Matson. The man delivered a five-by-seven brown envelope, waited while Barnes wrote a terse note on motel stationery and sealed it in another envelope, and was on his way back to St. Louis fifteen minutes later.

Barnes locked the door and sat at the table to examine the letter and photograph that had been faxed to Matson by an associate in Richmond. A cold exhilaration gripped him. The Mustang he'd seen parked at Kendra's apartment that afternoon was registered by the Commonwealth of Virginia to none other than Adam Case. He remained at the table for several minutes, studying every detail of the face in the photo, then got up and went to the phone. It was time to call Ross back into service.

WHEN ADAM RETURNED, he was carrying a blue nylon sport bag and a plastic sack from the twenty-four-hour convenience store-gas station. He'd taken time to shave. Jenna expressed her appreciation with a lingering kiss.

"What did Uncle Roy have to say?" she asked as she followed him to the dinette set.

"He'll put out an APB on the Olds Barnes was driving. Not that either of us thinks it'll do much good." He deposited both bags on the table and began unloading the one from the one-stop store. "Breakfast," he explained, lining up orange juice, a bag of bagels and a jar of instant coffee.

Jenna put the items away while he started unpacking the nylon carryall. "I meant to ask you earlier, where's your car?"

"In a deserted barn a couple miles outside town."

She turned in surprise, which skidded right into alarm when she saw what Adam had taken out of the bag.

"It was stupid of me to park it here earlier," he added, unaware of her reaction as he dropped a couple of shirts and an unopened package of boxer shorts on one of the chairs. "Barnes or Ross could have seen it and traced the plate number, and I'd prefer not to let them know I'm in the neighborhood." His gusty sigh carried the sound of self-reproach. "My only excuse is that I had other things on my mind at the time—such as worrying that you'd take one look at me and run like hell."

He glanced up, a rueful smile lifting one side of his mouth. The smile lasted roughly two seconds. "Jenna?"

She gave herself a little shake. "Sorry. I just—It didn't occur to me until now that you must have to use a gun sometimes."

"Rarely," Adam said. "In fact, almost never. But I am required to carry one in potentially hazardous situations." He hefted the larger of the two weapons he'd laid on the table. "And any confrontation with Dennis Barnes qualifies as potentially hazardous."

Jenna nodded, feeling a little foolish. If she'd thought about it at all, she'd have realized he would have to be armed on Sunday. She just wished he would put both weapons away until then. Especially the big one, the one that looked like it could blow a hole in a tank. Guns had always made her nervous.

"Is it loaded?"

"Yes. But it can't be fired unless I release the safety and pump a round into the chamber." He was watching her closely.

"Why do you have two guns?" she asked, not at all sure she wanted to hear the answer.

Adam placed the larger pistol back on the table and picked up the other one. Besides being smaller, it had a round cylinder like the six-shooters in cowboy movies. "This one's for you."

Jenna shook her head and unconsciously took a step backward in reflex. "Oh, no. I don't like guns."

"Of course you don't," he said, as if he, too, believed that no sane, reasonably intelligent person would have anything to do with them. Never mind that he personally owned at least two. "Unfortunately, at times a gun is the most effective way to deter violence. If someone is threatening you, you point a gun at him and nine times out of ten he'll back off." He paused, giving her a chance to admit that yes, that certainly made sense to her. She pressed her lips together and refused to utter a sound.

Adam stepped around the table. Jenna backed up another step, but that was as far as she could go. The sink was at her back, with the antique refrigerator on one side and the stove on the other.

"I *really* don't like guns, Adam."

"I don't expect you to adopt it, darlin'," he drawled.

She gave him a stern, uncompromising look. "I hope you don't expect me to handle it, either."

He kept advancing until they were only four or five inches apart. "You can't learn to use it without holding it." He spoke quietly, his voice calm but determined. "And don't bother telling me you have no intention of using it. I don't *want* you to use it. I hope to God you'll never have to fire a gun. Any gun. But you're going to learn to use this one, and you're damn well going to take it with you on Sunday."

"Do I have any say about this at all?" Jenna asked resentfully.

"Sure you do. If you flat can't bring yourself to touch this little peashooter, we'll just get in that big ol' Mercury parked outside and drive straight back to St. Louis. Tonight."

She observed that his drawl had become more pronounced as the message it conveyed got tougher. Sort of like putting cherry flavoring in cough syrup, she thought; the idea was to keep you from noticing the underlying bad taste.

"I'm glad I'm finding out now what a bossy son of a gun you are," she said, holding her hand out for the revolver.

There was a glint in Adam's eye as he shrugged and placed it on her palm. It didn't weigh as much as she'd thought it would. "What can I tell you, darlin'? I'm Texan to the bone."

Jenna snorted her opinion of such a lame defense, which earned her a grin.

"Okay, pay attention. This is a .22-caliber revolver. The bullets go in these little chambers. Unless you're practically on top of whoever you're shooting at, there's a good chance they'll just bounce right off without doing any real damage."

"Which, I presume, is why you referred to it as a peashooter," she muttered. "This is probably a dumb question, but why make me take it, if I can't blow anybody to smithereens?"

His grin flashed again. "It makes a nice loud bang."

Chapter Thirteen

There were no bullets in the .22, thank God. Unlike Adam's cannon, this gun didn't have any kind of safety mechanism. As he explained it, you pulled the trigger and a metal projectile exploded from the end of the barrel at a high enough velocity to damage whatever was in front of you. So long as it was directly in front of you, apparently, and didn't have a protective covering thicker than a sheet of notepaper. He said he would load the revolver Sunday morning.

"You mean you're not going to take me out and make me practice shooting things?" Jenna asked. She was still a little miffed at the way he was ordering her around.

"After dark? Hell, no. You might cripple somebody's dog."

She winced at the thought. "There's one thing you haven't mentioned, Tex. Where am I supposed to conceal this lethal weapon? I don't think it'll fit in my sock."

He reached into the nylon bag and pulled out one of the zippered fanny packs hikers and joggers use to carry their money and keys. It was a bright neon orange.

"This should do the job. You can wear it over your jeans."

"Okay," Jenna murmured. She didn't comment on the loud color. At least she would be highly visible.

Adam tucked the revolver and a box of bullets into the fanny pack. The corners of the box made conspicuous little peaks in the orange polyester, but she wouldn't be carrying extra bullets on Sunday.

"We can stick in a pack of tissues to camouflage the shape of the gun," he said as he returned the fanny pack to the blue tote.

"Or maybe a few gauze pads and something to use as a tourniquet," Jenna suggested.

Adam gave her a look, but didn't respond. He went to the couch and started stacking the cushions on the floor. "I'd say it's time for a hot bath and then bed."

Both sounded good to Jenna, especially the bed part. But his stubborn refusal to argue or even acknowledge her pique had only increased her resentment. She had a feeling she was cutting off her nose to spite her face, but she muttered, "I'm not tired."

Adam tugged open the couch and started pulling pillows and bedding from the top shelf of the closet. "Well, I am," he said mildly. "If you can stop sulking long enough, why don't you start running the bathwater."

Of course the request precluded another nasty comment. Jenna slunk into the bathroom without a word. She was sitting on the rolled edge of the huge old tub, leaning forward to test the water temperature with her fingers, when he came up behind her and—

with no warning and in a single smooth movement—
scooped her up and dumped her into the water.

Jenna shrieked, then sputtered, then grabbed the
edge of the tub, sat up and glared at him. Her mouth
fell open. Adam loomed over her, wearing a fiendish
grin and absolutely nothing else. Not a stitch. While
she, of course, was fully clothed except for her tennis
shoes, which fortunately she'd kicked off in the middle of his lecture on the care and feeding of .22-caliber
revolvers.

She gaped wordlessly as he climbed into the tub and
knelt astride her legs. He was smiling as he leaned
forward, lifted her chin with a finger and kissed her.

"I thought you needed cooling off," he murmured
against her lips.

"The water's hot," Jenna pointed out. And getting hotter by the second. "You're crazy. Certifi-
able."

Adam reached behind her to turn off the faucet.
"You want to see crazy? I'll show you crazy."

Her throaty laugh was abruptly choked off when he
grabbed her hips and yanked her under the water.

GORDON ROSS WAS BACK at the Utopia Motor Inn. His
assignment this time was to find a turquoise 1966
Mustang and the Justice Department investigator who
drove it, then make sure the man didn't interfere with
Dennis Barnes's plans.

He'd made one pass through town, which took all
of five minutes, but he hadn't seen the Mustang. He
figured he'd get a good night's sleep and start looking
in earnest tomorrow morning. The woman had ap-

parently turned in for the night. Her apartment was dark and the car she'd bought was parked in the drive.

As Ross got ready for bed, he decided to have breakfast at Eb's Café in the morning. Louise seemed to know everything that went on in Utopia. If there was a '66 Mustang in town, she could probably tell him not only where it was parked, but how much gas was in the tank and whether the owner wore boxer shorts or briefs.

ADAM WISHED HE'D THOUGHT to take the new clothes to the laundromat before wearing them. He adjusted the crotch of his jeans and told himself to be thankful the boxer shorts weren't as stiff as the blue chambray work shirt.

"Okay, I'm ready," Jenna announced as she emerged from the bathroom.

He settled the last cushion back on the couch and turned to find her smiling at him. It was a soft, intimate smile, a lover's smile, brimming with shared secrets. Adam gave a little get-over-here move of his head, testing her.

She came to him without a peep and wrapped both arms around his waist. But then she said, "That was a freebie. If you want an obedient female who'll bring you your slippers and curl up at your feet, I suggest you buy a collie."

He grinned down at her. "I don't wear slippers. I was just thinking, it's a good thing we'll be leaving after tomorrow."

"Oh? Why is that?"

"'Cause I doubt that bed would hold together long if we stayed."

"Degenerate," she said, stepping away to collect her purse. "We'd better get moving. I have to be back by ten-thirty."

Adam gave the sofa bed a last fond glance as he pulled the door closed behind them, thinking it was a wonder the thing hadn't fallen apart during the night.

They had been phoning Jesse Herron's number every five minutes since a quarter to six, but never got an answer. After stopping to fill the Mercury with gas and pick up several maps listing a variety of trails, they swung by Jesse's house before heading for the Garden of the Gods area. His truck wasn't there.

"Damn," Jenna said. "I bet he's still with Louise. Should we wait a while and try to catch him when he comes home to get ready for work?"

Adam shook his head. "We can't spare the time. Anyway, who's to say he didn't stop by and pick up a fresh uniform last night? He always comes to the café for lunch and dinner, doesn't he?"

"Every day since I've been here," she confirmed.

"Then I'll catch him there. Right now we need to reconnoiter the area he described to Barnes last night."

"And hope we don't run into Barnes in the process," Jenna muttered as he turned the car around in Jesse's drive. "I assume it's occurred to you that he might have the same idea—to do his reconnoitering early this morning."

"You assume right," he said. "Which is why I brought your friend, the cannon."

Jenna didn't reply, but her gaze went to the locked glove compartment, where the *cannon* rested in a smooth leather holster. She wished she'd never used that word to describe the gun, at least to Adam. Even

more, she wished knowing he planned to carry it on
their little scouting expedition didn't make her feel so
secure.

THE DEPUTY HAD PUT AWAY a stack of pancakes and
two eggs—over easy, swimming in grease—plus a half-
dozen sausage links and four slices of toast saturated
with butter. He'd washed everything down with three
cups of strong black coffee. Gordon Ross was glad he
didn't have the man's arteries.

He wished the deputy would stop spraying phero-
mones at Louise and go apprehend some tourists for
littering or spitting on the sidewalk. Ross had barely
managed to exchange a dozen words with her before
the lawman swaggered in and commandeered a table
near the kitchen. The second Louise spotted him, she
started preening and fanning the customers with her
heavily mascaraed eyelashes. They were obviously an
item, and Louise obviously wasn't going to say more
than "Would you like more coffee?" or "Will that be
all, sir?" to Ross or any other male customer until the
deputy left.

Ross checked his watch. Seven-oh-five. He sipped
at his lukewarm coffee and hoped a turquoise Mustang hadn't been zooming up and down Main Street
while he was cooling his heels in the café.

THE VIEW WAS MAGNIFICENT, awe-inspiring. It was
hard to believe they were only about four miles from
Utopia and less than two hundred from St. Louis.
Standing on top of an enormous rock outcropping, at
least twenty feet above the nearest treetop, Jenna
could almost imagine she'd stepped back in time a

hundred years or more and left civilization and all its trappings behind.

"Wow," she breathed. "Isn't this something?"

"It's beautiful," Adam agreed. "Pure, primitive wilderness."

"We could be the only two people on the planet."

He slipped an arm around her waist for a quick hug. "Unfortunately, we're not, and we still have a lot of ground to cover."

Jenna nodded and they began picking their way back down the irregularly terraced escarpment. This detour probably hadn't been a good idea, but neither of them had been able to resist checking out the view from the top. When they reached the base and made their way back to the trail they'd been following, Adam stopped to consult the map.

"Looks like Jesse plans a nice, easy hike for the two of you. The rendezvous point is only a couple hundred feet farther along this trail."

"You mean we won't be going up there?" Jenna said, tipping her head back and shielding her eyes with a hand to squint up at the natural stone obelisk. She sounded disappointed.

"If he suggests it, you'll suddenly develop a fear of heights," Adam replied. His voice had hardened and taken on an autocratic tone. "I mean it, Jenna. We have no way of knowing whether he and Barnes have had another little chat. They may have revised their plans since last night. How'd you like to come face-to-face with Dennis Barnes up there?"

She sobered at once. "I wouldn't."

"So no climbing anything more than ten feet high, right?"

"Right," Jenna agreed. The image of Barnes tossing her from the top of that tower of rock chilled her to the bone.

The utter isolation of this wildly beautiful place suddenly struck her. There was nothing but trees and rock, rock and trees, for what looked like miles in every direction. Without a map, or a compass and a crash course in orienteering, it would be all too easy to become hopelessly lost.

The success of Adam's plan depended on his making it to the rendezvous point Jesse Herron and Barnes had agreed upon before Barnes got there. But what if they *had* altered their strategy, picked a different place to meet?

What if Barnes had decided it would be safer to intercept Jesse's truck before he left the main road? What if Jesse showed up at her apartment—after Adam had left—and announced he'd changed his mind and they were going to a movie, or driving over to Crab Orchard Lake for a picnic?

"Having second thoughts?" Adam asked quietly.

The question startled her. She started to say no, but his dark, probing gaze saw too much. "Maybe one or two," she admitted. She pivoted in a slow circle, taking in the rough, breathtaking landscape that surrounded them, and unconsciously hugged her arms.

"You have to find Jesse," she said.

"I will," Adam promised. He slipped his arms around her from behind and she leaned back against his chest. His shoulder holster pressed into her upper arm. Jenna wished the feel of the warm, smooth leather was more comforting.

ROSS HEAVED A SIGH of relief when the deputy finally left. He'd been afraid he would have to eat a second breakfast to justify occupying the table any longer. The next time Louise made her rounds, he accepted a refill on his coffee.

"I didn't expect to see you back in town so soon," she said with a coquettish smile. Obviously Louise wasn't a one-man woman.

Ross gave her a roguish, bad-boy grin in return. "I didn't expect to be back so soon. But I found I couldn't stay away from a certain gorgeous waitress."

Her cheeks turned a pretty shade of pink, and she pretended she didn't believe his baloney for a second. But as soon as she got a free minute, she sat down at his table and asked how long he'd be staying this time. Just till tomorrow, Ross said, but he hoped to make it back next weekend.

As soon as he could work it in, he mentioned that a friend of his was supposed to drive over from Louisville, where he'd just spent a week on business. They planned to do some hiking, maybe a little rock-climbing—just relax and unwind for the rest of the weekend. His friend's name was Adam Case. At this point, Ross gave her a brief description of his old buddy Adam and casually added that he drove a '66 Mustang, light turquoise blue, a beauty of a car. Would she mind keeping an eye out for Adam, he asked, in case he was out enjoying the scenery when his friend arrived? Louise said no problem, she'd be glad to direct him to the motor inn if she saw him.

The response told Ross she hadn't already spotted the car, which meant it probably wasn't in town. A car like that would be noticed, and remembered. On the other hand, Barnes had said it *was* here, or had been, yesterday afternoon. Ross didn't relish the thought of telling his employer that both the car and its owner had apparently disappeared. He decided he'd have to check every garage, implement building, barn and tool shed in the vicinity. Preferably without getting caught. He hoped Louise's boyfriend would be occupied elsewhere for the rest of the day.

JENNA AND ADAM ARRIVED back at her apartment just before ten-thirty. She went straight to the café and he headed for the motor inn to see if he'd received any messages from Roy Stevenson. There was one. It read simply: "Call me, ASAP."

"The black Olds turned up here, early this morning," Roy told him right away.

A surprised frown shoved Adam's eyebrows together. "What! Are you sure?"

"Positive. It's the same plate number you gave me last night. The car belongs to Nolan Matson, the president of the bank where Jenna had the Kendra Jenner account."

"One of Barnes's money launderers," Adam remarked. "How the hell did the car get to St. Louis?"

"It's just a wild guess," Roy said dryly. "But maybe Barnes drove it here."

Adam didn't reject the possibility, but all his instincts told him Barnes was still in southern Illinois. "Where's the car now?"

"In the parking lot of Matson's bank. We're keeping an eye on it." Roy heaved a sigh of frustration. "I wish I could be more helpful, but at this point all we can do on this end is wait for Barnes to show himself. Right now nobody has any idea where he is."

Maybe not, Adam thought grimly, but I know where he'll be tomorrow afternoon. He didn't pass the information on to Roy, though. The last thing he wanted was for a mob of federal agents to suddenly descend on southeastern Illinois. Barnes had so many contacts, he'd know they were on the way before they piled into their government cars.

He said he'd be in touch when he had something new to report, then terminated the call. It was almost time for Jesse Herron to saunter into Eb's Café for lunch.

"I DON'T UNDERSTAND IT," Jenna said at a quarter past twelve. "He's always here by noon."

Adam gave her hand a surreptitious squeeze as she set a slice of cherry pie in front of him. He could see that Jesse's absence worried her. It worried him, too.

"Take it easy," he murmured. "He'll show up eventually. He's probably been so busy writing tickets and rounding up criminals he lost track of time, that's all."

Jenna made a cynical face. "Adam, the most dastardly criminals around here are teenagers who get their kicks switching road signs and using mailboxes for batting practice. I'm afraid he's deliberately avoiding me."

The possibility had occurred to Adam, too. He ate his pie while she went back to serving customers. Deputy Herron still hadn't appeared by twelve-thirty. When Jenna saw him push back his chair, she hurried over to the cash register.

"I hope you left me a nice gratuity," she said under her breath as she handed him his change.

"I thought I'd wait and give it to you tonight," he replied with a straight face.

She blushed and glanced around to see if anyone had heard. "Sounds good to me. What are you going to do about Jesse?"

"Go out and look for him."

She nodded. "Maybe you'd better take my car."

"Maybe I'd better not," Adam drawled. "In case he is avoiding you."

"Good point." He thought she might have said something more, but just then a perky blonde bounced into the café. Jenna mouthed the name *Louise*.

Adam stepped aside and took his time placing the bills she'd handed him into his wallet as the blonde approached the register.

"Hi, Susan," she chirped. "Big lunch crowd today?"

"About average. Jesse didn't come in, though."

Good girl, Adam thought.

"He didn't?" Louise was clearly surprised. "That's got to be a first. He was here for breakfast." She leaned against the counter with a self-satisfied smirk. "Maybe he decided to use his lunch hour to catch some Z's. He didn't get much sleep last night, if you know what I mean."

"I think I can guess," Jenna murmured. "I was just a little concerned that he might be under the weather."

"There was sure nothing wrong with him last night," Louise declared. "And this morning he put away a number-four breakfast and three cups of coffee. That man does love his coffee."

Adam contemplated the assortment of candy bars, gum and breath mints displayed next to the cash register as Jenna replied, "Well, I'm glad to hear he isn't ill."

"Oh, that's right!" Louise exclaimed, as if she'd been struck by a sudden flash of insight. "The two of you have a date tomorrow, don't you?"

"It isn't really a date. We're just going hiking at the Garden of the Gods."

"Better you than me," Louise said dryly. "Spending the afternoon climbing over filthy old rocks isn't my idea of a good time. The one and only time I was there I broke three nails and ruined a brand new pair of jeans." She examined her nails, as if to make sure they'd grown back, then added casually, "When I see Jesse tonight I'll be sure to tell him you were worried about him."

Adam saw Jenna glance at him from the corner of her eye. "You and Jesse are going out tonight?"

"More likely staying in," Louise said slyly. "And if it's anything like last night, I may have trouble getting to work on time in the morning. That's why I stopped by, to ask Eb if Nora ever let him know whether she'll be back tomorrow. She hadn't called when I left this morning."

"She'll be here," Jenna said. "She's scheduled for the breakfast and lunch shifts."

"Good, then I won't worry if I'm a few minutes late." Lowering her voice to a conspiratorial murmur, Louise added, "And there's no need to say anything to Eb. I'll deal with him when I come in tomorrow."

Jenna gave the other woman a thin smile. "Fine." Turning to Adam, she asked, "Can I help you with something, sir?"

He impulsively plucked a pack of gum from the rack, but before she could ring up the sale, Louise sidled between them and said, "Excuse me if this seems forward, but is your name Adam Case?"

Adam glanced at Jenna in time to see her mouth open in surprise. He thought she couldn't be any more stunned than he was. "Yes," he murmured. "I'm Adam Case."

"Oh, good, I thought you must be. Your friend described you to a T. He asked me to keep an eye out for you, in case he wasn't around when you got here."

"My friend?" Adam asked. All sorts of alarms were going off inside his head.

"Yeah—Gordon." Louise frowned. "I don't think he ever told me his last name. Tall guy, blond, blue eyes, good-looking."

"Of course. Gordon." Adam didn't dare look at Jenna again. "Gordon asked you to watch for me?"

"Uh-huh. He's staying at the motor inn up the street. You can't miss it, it's the only motel in town." Leaning around him, she glanced out the plate-glass window. "Where's your car? Gordon said it was a real beauty. My dad had a Mustang once, but he got smashed and totaled it."

"My car," Adam repeated. He felt like a stunned parrot. "It's at the motel. I already checked in."

"Oh." Louise gave him a pert smile. "I guess Gordon wasn't there, huh? Well, don't worry, you're bound to run into each other sooner or later. It's a small town."

He watched her flounce out the door, then turned to Jenna. Her face was pale and tense.

"She was talking about Gordon Ross, the man you said Barnes sent to watch me," she said. Adam admired the way she maintained her composure, despite the fact that she was obviously shaken.

"I don't know who else it could be," he admitted.

She started to say something else, but several diners picked that moment to approach the cash register. While Jenna dealt with them, Adam looked out the window and mulled over what Louise had said. When Jenna murmured his name, he turned back to face her.

"You know what this means," she said anxiously. "He knows your name. He knows what kind of car you drive. Dennis Barnes is after you now, too."

Adam didn't bother to contradict her. He'd come to the same conclusion.

Chapter Fourteen

By seven o'clock, Ross had investigated every garage in town and the four tool sheds that were large enough to conceal a 1966 Mustang. The damned car wasn't here.

The missing Mustang wasn't his primary concern, though. Dennis Barnes was. When Barnes sent someone to do a job, he expected the job to get done.

Ross retired to his cabin at the motor inn and stood under a cool shower for fifteen minutes to wash away his frustration and soothe his sunburn, then stretched out on the bed and tried to decide what direction to take next.

Okay, forget the car for now. Assume Adam Case is in town. He had to be staying somewhere. Not at the motor inn. If he was here, number one, the Mustang would be parked at one of the cabins; and number two, he'd have to venture out now and then, if only to get food. Besides Ross's cabin, two others showed signs of occupancy. He'd observed a young couple entering and leaving one, and a middle-aged woman carrying luggage into the other.

So where was Case staying? At the woman's apartment. Had to be. It was the only other possibility in this one-horse town. Ross threw on some clothes and left the cabin. He strolled by the café first to make sure she was still slinging hash. So far, so good.

But when he got within sight of the apartment, he realized *her* car was gone. He stopped in the middle of the street and scowled at the empty driveway.

ADAM THOUGHT HE MUST HAVE covered a couple of thousand miles of back-country roads in the last few hours. At least. Jesse Herron hadn't been on any of them. Nor was he at his house when Adam swung past on his way back to town.

Jenna had been right when she tried to tell him Barnes would anticipate and prepare for every possibility. Not only had he managed to keep them from getting to Jesse, he'd also discovered Adam's identity and that he was in the area. And now, in addition to Dennis Barnes and Jesse Herron, they had Gordon Ross to deal with.

But Barnes hadn't won yet, and Adam was determined that the only payoff for all his diligent scheming would be a prison cell. He'd underestimated Barnes, but that was a mistake he wouldn't make twice. And, just maybe, Barnes had underestimated him, too.

He left the Mercury parked next to his cabin at the motor inn, out of sight from the street, and set off on foot for Eb's Café. There wasn't much point in shopping and cooking for himself, and Jenna should be sitting down to her complimentary dinner about now. He observed that the Jeep he'd noticed yesterday morning was back, this time at the cabin two doors down from his.

HE TOLD HER OVER DINNER that he hadn't been able to find Jesse, but they tacitly agreed to postpone any serious discussion until Jenna got home. Adam had a hot bath waiting for her. This time he limited himself to washing her back.

"All right," she said when she was wrapped in a fluffy terry robe and comfortably settled at the opposite end of the sofa. "Where do we stand?"

Her calm composure surprised Adam. It also made his heart swell with pride. He hadn't been sure what to expect, how she would react to his failure to locate Jesse Herron. It suddenly hit him for the first time that the woman facing him wasn't the same woman he'd met in St. Louis. Her gaze was clear and steadfast. There wasn't a trace of the wariness and suspicion he'd noticed the first time he'd laid eyes on her.

Nor was she the woman who had run away a week ago, leaving behind everything but a stuffed dog and a couple of old pieces of ID in a desperate flight for survival. The woman facing him now with such amazing self-possession was strong, confident, determined. But then, he told himself wryly, he shouldn't be surprised. After all, she'd possessed the intelligence and the resolve to create Susan Devers and stage her own disappearance and death.

"As I see it, we've got two choices," he began. "I can get you out of town now, tonight—"

"That's not an option," Jenna interrupted. "So let's move on to number two."

Adam was momentarily taken aback. He'd suspected she might argue, but he hadn't expected her to veto the idea out of hand.

"No, dammit, let's stick with number one."

"Forget it, Adam," she said flatly. "I'm not slinking away in the dead of night and leaving you to take on Dennis Barnes, Gordon Ross and possibly Jesse Herron on your own. We do this together or not at all."

"And maybe die together?" he said, making his voice as hard and cold as he could.

"If it happens, it happens. Do you think I could live with myself if I ran away and *you* died?" She stopped and exhaled an impatient breath. "I can't run again, Adam. Please don't ask me to. You said yourself that if we don't deal with Barnes now, while we've got the chance, he'll just bide his time until he can catch me with my guard down."

He opened his mouth to argue, to refute his own words if that was what it took, but she stopped him with a raised hand.

"No, hear me out. The past five years of my life I've just *existed*—afraid to trust anybody, knowing every minute of every day that sooner or later he'd come after me. And then he did, and I finally took control of my own life again." She swiveled slightly, pulling one leg under her so that she faced him fully. "This past week has been terrifying. I had no idea where I'd end up, how I'd live, whether anyone was following me. But at least I knew I was *alive!* I was in control. Not Dennis Barnes, not the United States Marshals Service—*me!*" She raised her right hand and tapped her chest for emphasis. "And I figured out a few things along the way. I like making my own decisions, I'm perfectly capable of taking care of myself, and I'm stronger than I ever imagined I could be."

When she paused for breath, Adam drawled, "Are you finished?" Halfway through her fervent speech, he'd abandoned the idea of convincing her to leave. She was right: it was her life. He couldn't dictate how she should live it; he could only do his best to preserve it. And hope that when this was all over she might let him share it.

She gave him an uncertain, slightly suspicious look. "That depends. Are you going to argue with me or try to boss me around again?"

"No." He scooted across the lumpy, faded cushions. "I'm going to give you that gratuity I promised at lunch, and then I'm going to tell you about Plan B."

Plan B was that they would wait until she and Jesse entered the Garden of the Gods area to spring the truth on him. Adam would intercept them before they reached the rendezvous point Jesse and Barnes had arranged, flash his Justice Department ID, and they'd give Deputy Herron a quick, down-and-dirty synopsis of Dennis Barnes's sordid history, including the fact that he was at that moment violating the conditions of his recent parole.

If Gordon Ross made an appearance, Adam figured he would probably be with Barnes. Hopefully, by the time they encountered either man, Jesse would be on their side and the good guys would outnumber the bad guys. If Jenna suspected at any point before they encountered Adam that something wasn't right, or if she realized that Jesse had changed their destination, she would tell him the whole story and convince him to talk to Adam. And if that didn't work, she would jump out of his truck and run like hell.

"Have we thought of everything?" Jenna asked when they'd gone over the plan several times. They were wrapped in each other's arms on the sofa bed. "Everything we can reasonably hope to have any control over, I mean?"

Adam ran his hand through her short, silky hair. "I think so. I guess we'll find out tomorrow."

She burrowed into his chest and hugged him hard. "In case things get hectic and I don't have a chance to tell you, I love you."

Adam had to swallow before he could say the words to her. He wasn't sure if the emotion that clogged his throat was love, fear, or equal parts of both.

DENNIS BARNES LEFT the motel in Harrisburg for the last time at ten twenty-five Sunday morning. He had allowed more than enough time to reach the rendezvous point and settle in. Any nature lovers or hikers probably wouldn't start showing up until early afternoon, but it would be foolish to risk running into someone. Especially, he thought with a twisted smile, since he'd be carrying a loaded gun.

The three-year-old Dodge that Nolan's employee had driven down from St. Louis Friday night didn't handle or ride as well as the Olds. The suspension definitely needed work. Barnes wished he hadn't exchanged cars. There'd been no need; it was doubtful that anyone other than Jesse Herron had seen him driving the Olds.

When he made the turn south, he felt his heart rate start to speed up. Almost there. Five years he'd waited for this day, yearned for it with a hunger that was almost sexual in its intensity. Just a couple more miles, and suddenly there it was—the turnoff Jesse had told him to watch for. He pulled the Dodge into an obviously seldom-used lane that tortured the car's already defective suspension.

SUNDAY HAD DAWNED SUNNY and warm, a perfect day for puttering in the garden, riding a bicycle along quiet country lanes or clambering over primordial rock formations. Adam and Jenna were up early, first trying to reach Jesse Herron by phone, and then, when there was no answer, driving out to his house. Neither of them was surprised that he wasn't home.

"It was worth a shot," Adam said as they headed back to town.

"I wish I knew where Louise lives," Jenna muttered. "Or that she was at least listed in the phone book."

Sensing her increasing restlessness, Adam lifted his arm in invitation. She unfastened her safety belt and slid across the seat, pressing close to him.

"It isn't too late to change your mind," he said softly.

"I'm not going to change my mind. I just wish it was over with. It's the waiting that's hard."

"It's the waiting that's *hell*," he corrected, and ducked his head to kiss her hair.

When they got back to town, Adam decided not to bother taking the Mercury to the motel. Jesse was supposed to pick Jenna up at twelve-thirty. Neither of them said a word, but each knew what the other was thinking as Jenna put the key in the lock. Adam reached for her as his heel caught the door and kicked it shut. She fell into his arms, and they fell together onto the unmade bed.

He intended to take it slow and easy, a sensuous, loving pilgrimage, but in a matter of seconds he caught her impatience. Clothes were tugged, yanked, rent and finally thrust aside to the accompaniment of muttered curses and eager moans. Flesh sought flesh, stroking, rubbing, clutching and kneading, slipping and sliding in a frantic, unchoreographed ballet that made up in joyous exultation what it lacked in elegance.

It was some time before either of them could move, still longer before their breathing returned to normal. Eventually the awareness of passing time drove Adam to gently untangle their limbs and reach for his clothes. It was almost time for him to leave. But first he had to say what had been on his mind since Friday afternoon, when she'd walked through the door and he realized he would never again own his heart.

"When this is over, and you've got your life back, we need to have a serious talk." He kept his face averted, but he felt the bed shift and heard the soft rustle of the sheets as she got up.

"About what?"

He only hesitated a second, but it felt like a year. "The future." There, he'd said it. It was out in the open, where she could examine it, think about it....

"Whose future?"

He dropped the boot he'd been about to tug on and pivoted sharply. "What do you mean, whose? Ours!"

Jenna smiled at him from the bathroom door. "Oh. All right. I'll be happy to discuss our future, whenever you think you're ready."

She ducked into the bathroom and closed the door before he could think of anything to say. A minute later he heard the sound of water gushing into the tub. A wry smile took possession of his mouth as he reached for the boot he'd dropped. Whenever *he* thought *he* was ready!

He slipped into the bathroom just long enough to kiss her goodbye and then left. Suddenly he was anxious to put this day behind him, and Dennis Barnes with it. Jenna was right. He'd been obsessed with Barnes, for far too long. But no more. From now on, the only obsession in his life would be a woman with gold-flecked eyes and too many names. Someday soon, he would have to see if he could get her to settle on just one.

ROSS HAD BEEN HALF-ASLEEP when Adam collected the Mercury from the motor inn that morning. He was standing in front of the window, stretching himself into sensibility, when he saw the car turn into the street. By the time he pulled on a pair of pants and got out to the Jeep, the Mercury was long gone.

He'd hurried over to watch the woman's apartment, parking the Jeep around the corner and concealing himself behind a gigantic maple tree in the yard of an abandoned house across the street. He didn't have to wait long. About forty minutes later, the Mercury pulled into the driveway, and Adam Case and the woman got out and went into the apartment.

Ross moved the Jeep so he'd be able to sit in it and watch the apartment's front door. Barnes's instructions had been clear: Watch Case and keep him from interfering with his plans. Ross didn't know exactly what Barnes's plans were, only that they involved revenge for the part the woman had played in sending him to prison. But considering the severity of her crime, he expected she would soon meet a violent end. He doubted that Barnes knew she and Adam Case were lovers. Not that it would have made any difference. If Barnes had decided to kill her, she would die.

And I'm the one who'll have to deal with the boyfriend, Ross thought. The prospect neither troubled nor excited him. It was just a job.

They were in the apartment quite a while. Ross was just wondering if it would be safe to duck over to Eb's Café, have Louise get him a cinnamon roll and a cup of coffee to go, when Adam Case came out. He was carrying a small blue athletic bag, which he tossed onto the Mercury's front seat before sliding behind the wheel and driving off. Without the woman. Ross swore under his breath as he turned the key in the ignition. Apparently he'd be doing without breakfast this morning.

JESSE ARRIVED EXACTLY at the appointed time. Jenna was startled by his appearance. Either Louise hadn't let him get a wink of sleep the past two nights or something was really troubling him, eating him up inside. A guilty conscience, maybe? Jenna hoped so.

"Are you sure you want to do this?" she asked as they walked to his truck. If he caught her hidden meaning, he gave no sign. "You look like you might be coming down with something."

"I'm fine," he assured her, but his smile was a pallid imitation of the no-holds-barred stunner he usually uncorked. "I've been looking forward to today."

Jenna wondered nervously if he was serious, or just being polite. It was hard to gauge his mood. He didn't have much to say, which was unusual in itself, and when he did utter a few syllables, it was almost always in response to a question she'd asked about the place they were headed.

She paid close attention to conspicuous landmarks and the few signs she saw, and quickly realized that Jesse wasn't taking the same route she and Adam had followed yesterday. As far as she could tell, though, they were headed in the right direction, so she didn't panic. The revolver pressed against her left hip, conferring a confidence and sense of security she knew she had no business feeling.

"I hope you don't expect me to do any real rock-climbing," she said after a prolonged silence, deciding she'd better get that established early.

Jesse shook his head, but kept his eyes on the road. "I thought we'd just make this a nice, relaxing Sunday-afternoon hike. Nothing too demanding this time."

"That's good. I think I neglected to mention that I'm afraid of heights."

Nothing too demanding *this time*. That sounded promising, like he intended that there would be a next time. Had he already changed his mind about turning her over to Barnes? Or was he just trying to keep her relaxed and at ease, so she wouldn't suspect anything until it was too late?

"Here we are," Jesse suddenly announced. A few seconds later he steered the truck onto a narrow, rutted dirt lane that Jenna knew she had never seen before, much less ridden along. Alarm leapt in her breast.

"Are you sure you didn't make a wrong turn somewhere?" she asked, striving to sound normal. "This doesn't look like much of a road."

"It is a little rough," he allowed, as the truck jounced from rut to pothole and back. "It used to be an old logging road. Not many people know about it."

Jenna was positive Adam didn't. Her left hand instinctively sought the hard outline of the revolver, while the right groped for the handle of the door. Not that she planned to jump out now; she'd probably be pitched under the truck's wheels or headfirst into the trunk of a tree. But if she decided to move, she wanted to be able to do it quickly.

"Will this road take us to the Garden of the Gods area you were telling me about?" she asked, and prayed the answer was yes.

"Sure," Jesse replied. Jenna's muscles went slack in relief, then tensed up again a second later when he added, "Only we'll be coming in from a different direction, directly opposite the entrance most people use."

"From the back, you mean?" she said, hoping the rattling and grating noises from the truck obscured the nervousness in her voice.

"In a manner of speaking."

Jenna forced herself to take several slow, deep breaths. All right, she was in a bit of a jam. No need to go to pieces. Adam would be watching the access road everyone customarily used; everyone but Jesse Herron, that was. Right now he was waiting somewhere between the parking area and the tower of rock they'd climbed yesterday—had it really been only yesterday?—expecting her and Jesse to come strolling along any minute.

And they were how far away? Miles? Not coming toward Adam, but behind him.

Which meant that Dennis Barnes was probably also behind him, assuming Barnes hadn't changed his plan.

"This is where we leave the truck," Jesse remarked. She glanced around with a start and realized the lurching and jouncing had stopped. "Did I tell you this was beautiful country?" he asked as he opened his door and stepped down from the cab.

Jenna followed suit. "Yes. You did, and it is." He'd parked in an elevated area that provided a stunning view, mostly of towering, centuries-old trees. She was overwhelmed all over again, until gradually it dawned on her that none of the scenery before her looked familiar. Even if she could slip away from Jesse, she wouldn't have a prayer of finding Adam in this wilderness. So much for Plan B. And it was too late to run. She would have to tell Jesse about Barnes herself, and pray she could make him believe her.

Damn, why hadn't she thought to rehearse, or at least have Adam coach her? Instinct warned that if she just unloaded everything on Jesse now, suddenly and all at once, she'd sound exactly like the scheming, deceitful wife Barnes had described to him. She had to stay calm and rational, lay the whole story out from the beginning....

"We'll take this trail," Jesse announced. He started walking before Jenna could collect her thoughts, and she could do nothing but follow.

Chapter Fifteen

Something was wrong. It was no more than a ten-minute drive from Jenna's apartment. If Jesse had picked her up at twelve-thirty, as planned, they should have started hiking a half hour ago at the latest. It had taken Adam twenty minutes to reach this point, and he hadn't been pushing it.

Maybe Jesse had taken a different trail. It didn't make sense that he would have, unless he and Barnes had changed the rendezvous point, but all the other explanations that occurred to him were too intolerable to consider. Adam waited one more minute and then started retracing his steps.

He was leaning forward into a forty-five-degree rising incline, his right shoulder dropped slightly to compensate for the weight of the 9 mm Smith & Wesson on his left side, his eyes on the rock-strewn, uneven slope and his ears tuned for the sound of human voices. If he'd glanced up, just once, for half a second, he might have seen Gordon Ross in time to dodge the nightstick completely. Ross swung as if it was the bottom of the ninth, the bases were loaded and the count was three and two. Apparently he'd mistaken Adam's head for the ball.

Fortunately Ross was a southpaw, he was standing on the wrong side of the trail, and Adam was already listing in his direction. Adam instinctively tucked his chin to his chest and committed every ounce of his hundred and sixty-five pounds to a lunge to the right. The nightstick whacked his left shoulder blade a second before his right shoulder rammed into Ross's diaphragm. He heard something crack—bone or wood, he couldn't tell. It hurt enough to be bone. They went down together, rolling over branches, rocks the size of a man's fist and something that felt like either a rosebush or a porcupine before they separated and thumped to a halt at the base of the incline.

Adam's head might not have taken the brunt of the blow from the nightstick, but at some point on the way down it had collided with a small boulder. He struggled to overcome a nauseating dizziness and force his battered body to move. He remembered seeing a gun at Ross's waist.

There was a sound like a car backfiring close by, and a shower of dust and gravel exploded out of the rock next to his head. Stone splinters stung his cheek and neck. *Not a car, dummy. Ross's gun.* Adam managed to get his hands and feet under him and scrambled behind a huge cedar tree. As he fumbled with the snap fastener of his shoulder holster, Ross fired again. There was a soft *thwack* as more splinters whizzed past Adam's face.

He finally got the Smith & Wesson free, flipped the safety off, jacked a round into the chamber. Now, where was Ross? He waited for another shot, and when it came, threw himself to the right and squeezed off three rounds in the direction of the report. He scuttled behind another tree and hunkered down at its base, not stopping to see if he'd hit Ross.

When a minute had passed and Ross hadn't fired again, Adam chanced a quick look. The tall blond was sprawled on his back a dozen yards away, arms flung out and up as if in supplication. The gun was clutched in his left hand. He wasn't moving and didn't appear to be breathing.

Adam slowly rose to his feet and approached Ross as cautiously as if he were a napping grizzly. He kept the bore of the Smith & Wesson leveled at a point between Ross's eyes until he was close enough to kick the gun out of his hand, and even then he didn't relax until he saw the two holes in Ross's chest. One of them was perfectly centered over the heart.

Adam's legs suddenly didn't want to support him. He stumbled to a fallen tree and eased himself down. His head throbbed, the left side of his face felt like it had been attacked with a belt sander, and he ached in a hundred places. He lifted his hand to gingerly check his cheek. Most of the skin seemed to be there, but his fingers came away smeared with blood. All things considered, he decided he was in fantastic shape. That could have been him lying in a pool of his own blood.

He stared at Gordon Ross with a baffled frown. The man had been carrying a gun. Why in hell had he launched his attack with a club? The answer was obvious. Because clubs don't make as much noise as guns.

Jenna.

Adam lurched off the log and shoved the 9 mm back in its holster. Ross had attacked him to keep him from interrupting or interfering with Barnes's plans. Therefore, Barnes must not be far away. He would have heard the shots, and so would Jesse Herron and Jenna. How each of them had reacted would determine whether or not she survived until he could find her. He set off at a run for a familiar towering rock formation.

JENNA HAD ALMOST worked out how to begin her recitation when she and Jesse heard the sounds. They both stopped dead in their tracks.

"What the hell!" Jesse blurted. "Those were gunshots!"

Terror shot through Jenna. "Adam!" She started running as his name was torn from her on a cry of anguish.

Jesse caught her within seconds, grabbing her elbow and dragging her to a halt. She fought furiously to break free, but he had a grip like iron. "Let *go!* Please, Jesse, I have to go—"

"No, you don't. What you have to do is just calm down, Susan—or whatever your name really is. I can't let you go tearing off into the middle of a gunfight. For all we know it could be drug dealers, or two gangs shooting it out."

Jenna kicked his shin, hard, and when he yelped and relaxed his grip, she took off again. Through the trees she could see the huge rock outcropping she and Adam had climbed. The shots had come from that direction.

"Dammit, Susan, stop!" Jesse yelled as he came after her again.

"Jenna!" she yelled over her shoulder. "My name is Jenna Kendrick. There aren't any drug dealers or gangs within a hundred miles, you moron. That's an investigator for the United States... Department of Justice... being shot at...." She had to pause to catch her breath.

"A federal agent!" he hooted in disbelief. He'd fallen into step at her side, his long legs easily keeping pace with her shorter ones. The incredible claim incited him to reach out and grab her again. It was harder to stop her this time, because she had more forward impetus. He ended up swinging her in a circle before he managed to bring her to a stumbling halt.

"*Damn* you, Jesse!" She was frantic to get to Adam, but she had enough presence of mind to realize that Jesse was stronger and faster and she wasn't going anywhere until he decided to let her. She leaned forward, bracing her hands on her knees, and sucked air into her lungs while she whipped her emotions into line.

"His name is Adam Case," she said succinctly. "Like I said, he works for the Justice Department. He's trying to catch the man who told you I'm his runaway wife and paid you to deliver me to him." She straightened and stared straight into his astonished eyes, silently daring him to dispute a word of what she'd said.

"How did you know—"

"Mr. Case probably told her," a suave baritone interrupted.

Jenna whirled to face Dennis Barnes as he stepped from a small grove of trees.

"Somehow he found out about our agreement," he added. "And apparently the lovely lady here is working with him. Have I got it right, Kendra?"

"It's Jenna," she corrected. Her heart was trying to pound its way out of her body, but her voice was remarkably steady. "No, you don't have it right. I'm not working with anybody."

His smile was an ugly gash in a mask of hatred. "You lie so convincingly...Jenna. It's a pity I had to let Ross dispense with Mr. Case. I'd looked forward to dealing with him myself. Unfortunately I can't be two places at once, and you were a higher priority."

"I'm flattered," Jenna muttered. *Don't believe him. Don't believe a word he says.*

Jesse watched and listened intently, but he didn't seem inclined to join the conversation. She wished she knew what he was thinking, whether she could count on him.

"Don't be," Barnes said silkily. "Adam Case was business. He was only doing his job." He spread his hands in a magnanimous gesture. "Just business. The animosity I feel for you, on the other hand, is quite personal."

Jesse abruptly ended his silence. "You played me for a fool. You're not her husband, and she didn't steal any money from you."

"I did embellish the truth a little, it's true," Barnes admitted. While he addressed the other man, his frigid gaze never left Jenna's face. "She isn't and never has been my wife. She was my sister-in-law, once upon a time, and she did steal from me—my wife, my son and five years of my life."

"I gave testimony that sent him to prison," Jenna explained. "Where he'd still be, if he hadn't spent a lot of his dirty money to buy himself a parole."

"A *lot* of money," Barnes agreed. "And every penny well spent. It brought us both to this moment. My destiny—and yours."

He reached behind his back and produced a gun— not as big as Adam's, but every bit as deadly, Jenna was sure.

"Whoa!" Jesse exclaimed. Evidently the sight of the gun had reminded him that he was a law-enforcement officer. "Hold it right there, mister. Just take it easy. I'm still not a hundred percent sure what's going on here. Put the gun away and we'll talk it out. I don't care what kind of grudge you've got against the lady—you can't expect I'll stand here and let you shoot her."

"No," Barnes said quietly. "I never expected that, Deputy Herron." And he calmly pointed the gun at Jesse and fired.

Jenna recoiled violently, her horrified gaze flying to Jesse. His handsome features arranged themselves into a grotesquely astonished expression as he clutched his stomach with one hand and staggered forward. Barnes backed up, trying to avoid him. When he saw that he couldn't, he fired another bullet into Jesse's chest. The second round slowed but didn't stop him. Even half-dead, Jesse Herron was a strong man. He kept coming, that ghastly look of surprise still on his face. Barnes took another step backward and his heel caught on the root of a tree. He flailed both arms wildly to maintain his balance.

She didn't stop to think. As Jesse stumbled and fell into Barnes, Jenna ran for the rock outcropping.

She must have covered the length of a football field before she remembered the revolver in the fanny pack strapped around her waist. She groped for the zipper tab, couldn't find it. The pack had worked itself around to the middle of her back, probably when she was wrestling with Jesse. She didn't dare stop to re-arrange it. She knew without looking that Barnes was coming after her.

Her lungs were on fire. Sweat ran into her eyes, half blinding her. Every breath was a tortured sob, and she'd already developed a stitch in her right side. She swiped a hand across her forehead and kept running, trying to zigzag as much as she could without pulling herself off course. Sometimes the trees were so close together they blocked the column of stone, but a few feet farther on she would catch a glimpse of it and know she was still headed in the right direction.

She wiped sweat from her eyes again and reached back, trying to tug the pack around so she could get at the zipper. The extra exertion almost pushed her past her limits, but just when she thought she'd have to abandon the effort, the pack suddenly gave and slid around her waist. She yanked the zipper open a second before a shot rang out and a geyser of dirt and moldy leaves spouted a few feet to her right. She gave a choked cry and automatically swerved left.

Don't panic! a clear, cool voice admonished. *Shoot back at the son of a bitch!*

She removed the revolver from its hiding place and did exactly that. Over her shoulder. On the run. Not stopping or even slowing to take aim. Why bother, since Barnes would have to be virtually on top of her for the .22 to do any damage? She fired off two shots, thinking she'd better save a few bullets in case he didn't take the hint and go away. For a minute or so it seemed he actually might have. But then he fired again. His accuracy was improving. A chunk of bark flew out of a tree trunk and ricocheted off her upper arm as Jenna sprinted past. She flinched, stumbled, almost fell. Damn, how could he see her well enough to come so close?

She suddenly remembered the fanny pack's bright orange color. It might as well be a flashing neon arrow, pointing out every desperate, uncoordinated zig and zag she made. Using her free hand, she tried to separate the overlapping ends of the waistband. The Velcro strips held fast. Sobbing in frustration now, as well as fear, she jammed the revolver into the snug waist of her jeans, ripped the Velcro apart, then hurled the pack as far from her as she could.

Either the trail had ended or at some point she'd strayed from it. The ground had become rough and craggy, marked with narrow and not-so-narrow gullies and rock outcroppings—most no larger than a family sedan, some as big as a house—where the trees thinned before giving way to bare stone. The towering formation loomed ahead, closer but still a daunting distance away. Jenna wasn't sure she could make it. If she tripped and fell, she was afraid she wouldn't be able to get up again.

Adam, where are you? Please, God, let him be all right. And if I have to die, please let me find him first. Let me see him just one more time, know that he's alive and in one piece....

Maybe she didn't see the chasm because she was so distracted by fear and worry for Adam. Or maybe she did see it, but exhaustion had dulled her senses and slowed her reflexes so that her brain didn't process the information in time to stop. One second the soles of her tennis shoes were skidding across moss-covered rock, and the next she was sliding into nothingness. The drop was no more than seven or eight feet, but her ankles and knees felt the impact as if she'd jumped out of an airplane without a parachute.

When the pain had subsided a little, Jenna unclenched her jaw and sat up to assess the damage. Miraculously, there didn't appear to be a lot: a couple of raw places on her arms where the skin had been scraped away, a sore patch on her back that she couldn't see, but which didn't seem to be bleeding, and, of course, her ankles. She wondered numbly if one or both were broken.

There was only one way to find out if she could walk. Gritting her teeth, she inhaled a deep, fortifying breath, grabbed hold of a protruding chunk of rock on the wall of the fissure, just above eye level, and hauled herself up before she could lose her nerve.

It wasn't as bad as she'd feared. She could tolerate the pain, so long as she moved at a snail's pace and remembered to walk flat-footed. She didn't think either ankle was broken, not that that was any great consolation. Any way she looked at it, she was in a pretty desperate situation.

Dennis Barnes was still after her. Even if she could find a way out of this crevasse, she had no idea where Adam was or if he was in any condition to come to her rescue. And all she had to defend herself with was the peashooter, which she was surprised to find still wedged in the waistband of her jeans, and four bullets. She rested her head against the cool stone wall and fought against a crushing sense of hopelessness and defeat.

ADAM HAD JUST REACHED the base of the escarpment when he heard the first two shots, spaced seconds apart. He knew at once that they hadn't come from Jenna's .22. Shutting down the part of his mind that acknowledged pain and fatigue, he uttered a silent prayer and took off in the direction of the sounds.

A minute later there was a third report, followed by another stretch of silence and then a fourth shot. Adam was trying to decide what the silences meant when he heard two sharp pops. His heart gave an excited lurch. Those last sounds *had* been the .22. What's more, they'd been discernibly closer. He drew the Smith & Wesson and tapped the last reserves of his strength for an additional burst of speed.

JENNA HOBBLED SLOWLY and painfully along the uneven floor of the fissure, one hand braced on the wall for support, hoping to find something to grab hold of or stand on so she could climb out.

There was nothing, only the rough but unbroken stone walls. She hadn't spotted any clefts or cracks big enough to use for hand or footholds, and even at the narrowest places the walls were a good four feet apart.

If they'd been just a couple of feet closer together, she could have braced her feet and back against them and attempted to climb up that way. She didn't want to think about the strain such an attempt would put on her ankles, telling herself that at least she would have tried.

She stopped and leaned against the wall to rest for a moment, trying to estimate how much time had passed since she'd fallen into this miniature canyon. Probably no more than three or four minutes, though it felt like hours. Was Barnes still up there looking for her? Yes, of course he was. He'd invested too much time and effort in planning his revenge. He wouldn't give up so easily.

How long before he found the crevasse?

Maybe he'd stumble across it the same way she had, fall in and break both legs, or better yet, land on his head.

The thought made Jenna smile grimly. Now, that would be poetic justice. She fixed the image in her mind as she straightened and began moving again, using it to distract her attention from her aches and pains.

After a while she realized that the stone floor had begun to slope upward. At first she thought it was only her imagination, mere wishful thinking. But by the time she'd taken a dozen more steps, the shooting pain in her ankles confirmed that she was indeed walking uphill. Her spirits lifted as hopeful optimism replaced some of her misery. She peered ahead, lifting her gaze to the rim of the crevasse. Yes! Another few yards and she'd be able to reach the top of the wall and pull herself up and out.

They were the longest few yards she'd ever traveled. Longer than the walk from the courtroom doors to the witness stand and the stroll down the pungent hall to the deputy medical examiner's office combined. By the time she reached a point where she could curl her fingers over the top of the wall, both ankles felt as if someone had driven red-hot spikes through the bones. Jenna was afraid to look at them, but she knew they were badly swollen; she could feel the tops of her tennis shoes biting into her flesh.

She closed her eyes and inhaled deeply several times, trying to psych herself for the ordeal of scaling the wall. There was no way she could pull herself all the way up; she would have to use her feet to gain purchase against the stone. The anticipation of the agony to come almost defeated her before she began. Maybe she should stay down here. Maybe Barnes wouldn't find her. Maybe if she just kept going in the direction she had been, the floor of the crevasse would eventually rise to ground level.

But she couldn't go any farther, and this wasn't a hiding place, it was a trap. And Barnes *would* find her; if not today, then tonight, or tomorrow, or the next day. By then she'd be too weak to think, much less defend herself.

She checked to make sure the revolver was still securely tucked into the waist of her jeans, took one more deep breath, gritted her teeth and stretched her arms overhead. She groped along the top of the wall, searching for the best places to anchor her hands. Her fingertips encountered loose dirt, moss, sharp-edged rocks—

The smooth, supple texture of expensive leather.

Jenna threw her head back with a gasp as a strong hand closed around her left wrist.

"Let me help you," Dennis Barnes said with silky menace.

He was on one knee, leaning over the edge of the crevasse, so close that Jenna saw her own terror reflected in his eyes. His fingers tightened around her wrist, crushing the tender skin as he straightened and then stood upright. Her feet left the ground. Pain shot down her arm and the fingers of her left hand began to tingle, but her ankles suddenly felt immeasurably better.

"Just a few more feet," he said genially. His smile reminded her of a death's head. He turned his hand slightly, just enough to give her arm a vicious twist. A small cry of pain escaped her.

"No, don't thank me," he murmured. "It's my pleasure, I assure you."

The sadistic satisfaction in his voice hit Jenna like a blast of arctic air, shocking her into action. She let go of the rim and went for the revolver, shoving her right hand between her body and the wall, ignoring the pain when her knuckles scraped against the rough stone.

"What are you—" Barnes began as her fingers closed on the grip of the .22. The suspicion in his voice told her she didn't have much time. She slipped her index finger inside the trigger guard and tugged the revolver free, heard the metallic clink when the barrel grazed the wall and knew he heard it, too.

He released her wrist before she could bring the revolver up to fire. For a few eternal moments everything seemed to happen in slow motion. Jenna realized she was falling . . . saw his right hand move toward the small of his back . . . watched the gun in her own hand float up past her face, her finger curled around the trigger, beginning to squeeze. . . .

She didn't scream when the impact of landing ripped through her ankles, but only because the pain stole her breath. Her finger jerked on the trigger as her knees buckled, and an instant later her head bounced off the wall behind her.

Jenna lay at the bottom of the crevasse, dazed and in too much pain to move, and watched helplessly as Barnes leveled his gun at her. His death's-head grin had become a feral snarl. The trickle of blood from his left temple gave her scant satisfaction. It was a measly little scratch, no big deal, just enough to enrage him. This was it; she'd blown her only chance. He was going to kill her now, and there wasn't a thing she could do to stop him. She didn't even have the strength to lift her arm and try to get off another shot.

She resisted the desire to close her eyes, forcing herself to stare at the dark bore of the gun. When the shot came, she flinched in involuntary reflex, her entire body clenching, waiting for the pain to hit. When it didn't come, she wondered giddily if she was already dead. Maybe her skull had cracked like an eggshell when it smacked into the wall.

But if she was dead, why did she still hurt so much?

And then she noticed the bright red circle that had blossomed on the front of Barnes's shirt. No . . . wait . . .

A sonorous voice competed with the ringing in her ears, yelling an insistent summons from above. *"Jenna!"*

Yes, she was definitely dead. Now she was hearing angels. But something wasn't right. The peashooter had only nicked the side of Barnes's head. Why was there blood on his shirt? And his gun—it wasn't pointed at her anymore. As she watched, it dangled from his hand, then dropped into the crevasse, missing her left foot by inches. Her stunned gaze followed the weapon's descent and flew back up in time to see Barnes sink out of sight, as if the ground had suddenly opened and swallowed him up.

"*Jenna!* Dammit, answer me!"

Jenna closed her eyes and prayed the voice wasn't an hallucination. Angels didn't snarl, did they? Or swear?

"Are you hurt?"

And surely their voices didn't crack with emotion. She opened her eyes and twisted painfully, craning her neck to see the top of the wall she was leaning against. The figure lying on his stomach and glaring down at her wasn't an angel. Yet. But he looked like he wasn't far from qualifying.

"Adam! Your face—"

"Are you *hurt?*" he repeated fiercely.

"Yes," she said with a grimace.

"Oh, God. Where?"

Her laugh came out sounding more like a sob. "Everywhere. I feel like I was run over by a bus."

He closed his eyes for a moment. "Barnes didn't shoot you?"

Jenna shook her head and immediately regretted the gesture. "No," she said weakly. "I'm just really banged up. I don't think anything's broken, but I can't climb out of here."

Adam's relief was written on his face. "Okay, just hold on. I'll get you out."

He removed his belt and used it to pull her up until he could grasp her arms and lift her the rest of the way. They collapsed onto the ground, each insisting on examining the other's injuries between frantic kisses and solicitous caresses, both talking at once and not very coherently.

"Is it really over?" Jenna asked when she'd satisfied herself that, appearances to the contrary, Adam wasn't about to expire and hadn't, in fact, suffered any permanent damage.

He tenderly stroked her cheek. "It's really over," he said solemnly. "Dennis Barnes will never again be a threat to you or anybody else. You have your life back, Jenna."

She smiled and looped her arms around his neck as he swept her up in his arms and started the long trek back to where he'd left the Mercury.

Epilogue

Fortunately Adam didn't have to carry her the entire distance. They were intercepted by a trio of park rangers and spent the rest of the afternoon explaining first the gunfire that had been reported by several alarmed tourists and then the three dead bodies that had turned up. But when their statements had been taken and they were finally on their way back to the cramped apartment in Utopia, she remembered his solemn declaration.

You have your life back.

Incredible as it seemed, it was true. It was *her* life now, to live and use and explore as she pleased. The future stretched ahead like an empty highway. So many choices to make . . . and so many decisions.

The first and most important decision was also the easiest, by far. Jenna was eager to begin the journey ahead of her, but she didn't want to make it alone. The trouble was, she had no idea how a woman went about asking a man to spend the rest of his life with her. Especially when the man was an independent, strong-willed Texan who was used to going his own way and living life on *his* terms.

Three days later she still hadn't come up with a way to broach the subject. And she was more than a little annoyed with Adam because he hadn't. After all, he was the one who had first referred to it as *their* future. Had he changed his mind?

They were sitting on the floor of the living room in Jenna's rented house, devouring trays of Mexican take-out food while they waited for *The African Queen* to start on one of the cable channels. A couple of hours earlier, they'd finally finished giving the last in an exhausting series of depositions. Jenna had grown increasingly restless since then. She knew that as soon as Adam had signed the last copy of the last deposition, his business here was officially finished.

They'd spent the past three days and nights together, and every minute of the time had been wonderful, their various contusions, abrasions and lacerations notwithstanding. But Adam hadn't given any indication that he planned to stay in St. Louis or dropped any hints that he'd like to take her with him when he left. If they were going to have that "serious talk" about the future he'd mentioned Sunday morning, it looked as if she would have to initiate it. She reached for a nacho chip and tried to figure out how to begin.

While she pondered, Adam finished off his burrito, wiped his fingers on a napkin and announced, "Okay, I'm ready."

She looked at him in question. "Ready for what?"

He didn't answer until he'd switched to a more comfortable position, leaning back against the sofa with his long legs stretched out and crossed at the ankles. "To discuss our future."

"Oh." Jenna had a little trouble swallowing the corn chip. She took a fast sip of soda and set her unfinished dinner aside. "All right."

"I've given it a lot of thought the last few days," he murmured.

Jenna didn't reply. This was news to her. She could have sworn the only things on his mind had been making love and dictating sworn statements. But the next words out of his mouth were even more surprising.

"First we need to think about giving you a new identity."

"*Another* one?" she asked with a groan. "You can't be serious. I've already got so many names I had trouble remembering which one to sign on all those depositions."

He was sympathetic, but firm. "This would be the last time. Promise."

Jenna started to strenuously object. But something in his voice stopped her. And then she noticed the warm, ardent gleam in his eyes. Her heart fluttered giddily, but she strove to keep her expression composed and her tone calm.

"Would I at least get to pick the name?"

"Well, actually, I have one in mind. I was sort of hoping you'd like it."

The flutters became wild palpitations. Jenna pretended to consider the idea as she shambled across the carpet on her knees and collected Adam, Jr., from a corner of the sofa.

"I hope it isn't something hard to pronounce . . . or spell," she said as she settled down beside him. Close beside him, her shoulder and hip touching his.

"Not at all." He slipped an arm around her waist and pulled her closer. "In fact, it's one of your more ordinary names. Plain vanilla, four letters, one syllable."

Jenna waited, idly running her fingers over the basset hound's plush fur, determined not to blurt out an answer until he'd asked the question. Her lips curved in a secretive smile as she stroked the hound's stomach. The certified checks she'd sewn inside would pay for an apartment full of new furniture, starting with a king-size bed. There might even be enough left over for a honeymoon cruise....

Her fingers strayed to Adam, Jr.'s neck, and she suddenly froze, then snatched him up for a closer look. Her eyes flew open wide.

"Adam!"

"That's two syllables, darlin'," he pointed out.

Jenna was too busy fumbling with the red satin ribbon that had replaced the hound's velvet collar to bother with a reply. Removing his arm from around her waist, Adam reached over and tugged an end of the bow, smoothly palming the emerald-cut diamond ring it had secured before she could grab it.

"The name I had in mind is Case," he said as he lifted her left hand. He held the ring poised at the end of her third finger. The teasing note was gone from his voice. His warm brown gaze was solemn. And just a little uncertain? "I know these past few days have been pretty chaotic. You haven't had much chance to think about what you want to do now, how you want to spend the rest of your life. I should probably give you a little more time, but—"

"I've had all the time I need," Jenna interrupted softly. "How I spend the rest of my life isn't nearly as important as who I spend it with."

"You're sure about that?" Yes, she'd been right about the uncertainty—it was in his voice, too.

"Positive." Jenna put all her conviction, all her hope and faith and love, into the answer. Then, in case he still needed convincing, she added, "Of course, it would have to be someone with a romantic soul. The kind of man who'd give a woman stuffed animals and huge bouquets, take her on moonlight cruises, rescue her from homicidal maniacs...."

The dimple in his right cheek flashed briefly. It was an endearing contrast to the bruised and scratched left side of his face. And then he suddenly moved, changing position again so that he was facing her literally on one bent knee.

"In case I haven't made it clear by now, I'm absolutely crazy, out-of-my-head in love with you," he said in the deep, tender drawl that never failed to melt her bones. "I don't want to think of going to bed at night or waking up in the morning or growing old and gray without you next to me. Marry me, Jenna. Take my name or pick another one, but please say you'll share my life."

She waited a moment before she answered, but even so her voice was tremulous. "Yes, to all of it. I want to be Jenna Case, as soon as possible and for the rest of my life."

Adam's smile was blinding as he slipped the ring on her finger. It fit as perfectly as the new name he'd given her, as the life he'd given her.

A few minutes later she remembered that she'd destroyed all her Jenna Kendrick identification when she became Susan Devers. Wouldn't she need it to apply for a marriage license?

She decided not to mention that little problem just yet. Adam was demonstrating a talent she was sure he hadn't picked up at the Justice Department, and she was reluctant to distract him. Surely Uncle Roy would be able to restore her old new identity before she assumed the next new one. The last one.

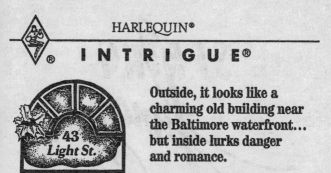

Harlequin proudly presents four stories about
convenient but not *conventional* reasons for marriage:

- ◆ To save your godchildren from a
  "wicked stepmother"

- ◆ To help out your eccentric aunt—and her sexy
  business partner

- ◆ To bring an old man happiness by making him
  a grandfather

- ◆ To escape from a ghostly existence and become a
  real woman

Marriage By Design—four brand-new stories by four
of Harlequin's most popular authors:

CATHY GILLEN THACKER
JASMINE CRESSWELL
GLENDA SANDERS
MARGARET CHITTENDEN

Don't miss this exciting collection of stories about
marriages of convenience. Available in April, wherever
Harlequin books are sold.

When the only time you have for yourself is...

Spring into spring—by giving yourself a March Break! Take a few *stolen moments* and treat yourself to a Great Escape. Relax with one of our brand-new stories (or with all six!).

Each STOLEN MOMENTS title in our Great Escapes collection is a complete and never-before-published *short* novel. These contemporary romances are 96 pages long—the perfect length for the busy woman of the nineties!

Look for Great Escapes in our Stolen Moments display this March!

SIZZLE by Jennifer Crusie
ANNIVERSARY WALTZ
by Anne Marie Duquette
MAGGIE AND HER COLONEL
by Merline Lovelace
PRAIRIE SUMMER by Alina Roberts
THE SUGAR CUP by Annie Sims
LOVE ME NOT by Barbara Stewart

Wherever Harlequin and Silhouette books are sold.

HARLEQUIN®

Don't miss these Harlequin favorites by some of our most distin-
guished authors!
And now, you can receive a discount by ordering two or more titles!

HT#25409	THE NIGHT IN SHINING ARMOR by JoAnn Ross	$2.99	☐
HT#25471	LOVESTORM by JoAnn Ross	$2.99	☐
HP#11463	THE WEDDING by Emma Darcy	$2.89	☐
HP#11592	THE LAST GRAND PASSION by Emma Darcy	$2.99	☐
HR#03188	DOUBLY DELICIOUS by Emma Goldrick	$2.89	☐
HR#03248	SAFE IN MY HEART by Leigh Michaels	$2.89	☐
HS#70464	CHILDREN OF THE HEART by Sally Garrett	$3.25	☐
HS#70524	STRING OF MIRACLES by Sally Garrett	$3.39	☐
HS#70500	THE SILENCE OF MIDNIGHT by Karen Young	$3.39	☐
HI#22178	SCHOOL FOR SPIES by Vickie York	$2.79	☐
HI#22212	DANGEROUS VINTAGE by Laura Pender	$2.89	☐
HI#22219	TORCH JOB by Patricia Rosemoor	$2.89	☐
HAR#16459	MACKENZIE'S BABY by Anne McAllister	$3.39	☐
HAR#16466	A COWBOY FOR CHRISTMAS by Anne McAllister	$3.39	☐
HAR#16462	THE PIRATE AND HIS LADY by Margaret St. George	$3.39	☐
HAR#16477	THE LAST REAL MAN by Rebecca Flanders	$3.39	☐
HH#28704	A CORNER OF HEAVEN by Theresa Michaels	$3.99	☐
HH#28707	LIGHT ON THE MOUNTAIN by Maura Seger	$3.99	☐

Harlequin Promotional Titles

#83247	YESTERDAY COMES TOMORROW by Rebecca Flanders	$4.99 ☐
#83257	MY VALENTINE 1993	$4.99
	(short-story collection featuring Anne Stuart, Judith Arnold,	
	Anne McAllister, Linda Randall Wisdom)	

(limited quantities available on certain titles)

	AMOUNT	$
DEDUCT:	10% DISCOUNT FOR 2+ BOOKS	$
ADD:	POSTAGE & HANDLING	$
	($1.00 for one book, 50¢ for each additional)	
	APPLICABLE TAXES*	$ _____
	TOTAL PAYABLE	$ _____
	(check or money order—please do not send cash)	

To order, complete this form and send it, along with a check or money order for the
total above, payable to Harlequin Books, to: **In the U.S.:** 3010 Walden Avenue,
P.O. Box 9047, Buffalo, NY 14269-9047; **In Canada:** P.O. Box 613, Fort Erie, Ontario,
L2A 5X3.

Name: _____

Address: _____ City: _____

State/Prov.: _____ Zip/Postal Code: _____

*New York residents remit applicable sales taxes.
Canadian residents remit applicable GST and provincial taxes.

HBACK-JM